Introducing
Shirley Braverman

Introducing Shirley Braverman

Hilma Wolitzer

Farrar Straus Giroux NEW YORK

Library of Congress Cataloging in Publication Data
Wolitzer, Hilma   Introducing Shirley Braverman
I. Title   PZ7.W8337In   [Fic]   75-25872

For my mother and father

Introducing
Shirley Braverman

one

The Basement

The sirens went off just as I was coming to the best part of the book, the chapter where the heroine discovers that her new friend is really her long-lost sister. "Oh, for heaven's sake," I said, trying to read a few more lines.

But my father was putting his white helmet on, and that whistle around his neck that always reminded me of gym teachers. "Hurry up," he said. "Come on, children! Etta!" he called to my mother, who was very neat and couldn't go down to the air-raid shelter until she was sure the seams of her stockings were straight.

This all happened during World War II when my father was the air-raid warden for our street. If anyone left even a single twenty-five-watt bulb on during a black-out, when it was supposed to be completely dark, my father blew on his whistle until he was red in the face. He would mutter about enemy planes finding Brooklyn someday because of one little light and about how we all had to cooperate and stick together.

My little brother, Theodore, who didn't like loud noises, and especially sirens, was hiding under the kitchen table, and my older sister, Velma, couldn't be found anywhere.

"Velma!" my father shouted. "Where is that girl? The war will be over before we get downstairs."

I knocked on the bathroom door. "Velma? Are you in there? You better hurry up. Can't you hear the sirens?"

The door opened and someone with a green face was looking back at me.

"Well, don't just stare," Velma said.

"Wh—what happened to you?"

"Nothing *happened,* baby. It's just a beauty mask. A person can't have any peace or privacy in this place." She was rubbing her face with a towel all the time she was talking.

"The towel's getting green," I said.

"Nobody *asked* you," Velma said, turning red under the green.

Daddy blew two short blasts on his whistle. "Let's go, everybody." He reached his hand under the table to Theodore. "Come on, Ted, old sport. Nothing to be afraid of."

Finally we were all out in the hallway with our neighbors and Daddy led us to the air-raid shelter, which was really the basement of our apartment building, a place that scared the life out of me.

Of course I wasn't too scared then, when everyone in the building was there together. We all stayed very close to one another and the grownups made funny jokes and sang songs to keep the children cheerful, so we wouldn't think about enemy planes and bombs and things like that. Some of the women formed a little group and talked about their children and about recipes and food prices, just as if they were sitting on a park bench in the sunshine. Old Mr. Katz from apartment 4J told corny jokes and riddles. "What has four wheels and flies?" he asked.

"What does?" said Mrs. Katz, even though she had heard all his jokes a million times.

"A garbage truck!" Mr. Katz yelled, and he laughed so hard that he didn't notice everyone else was groaning.

I had to hold Theodore's hand and he held on so tight that my hand got all hot and sticky.

"I'll just die if anyone sees me," Velma whispered to Mother.

"You look fine," Mother said, "perfectly fine," even

though there was still a little green around Velma's eyes and on her chin.

I looked around me at the gray walls and I shivered. That basement held in its shadows every horror it was possible to imagine. *Never, never* go down in the basement alone, we were warned. But I hardly needed a warning. I wouldn't go down there alone, even on a dare. What lurked, what waited with perfect patience for us? The Mummy waited, or perhaps just his hand, floating in space. Mr. Hyde waited, or worse still, Dr. Jekyll, who at the very moment he saw us would become Mr. Hyde. Heh, heh, heh. Janitors waited, nameless, faceless janitors famous for their torture of children stupid enough to wander into basements. Witches, bogeymen, murderers, Ali Baba's thieves, Heidi's wicked aunt, Captain Hook, vicious dogs, dead bodies . . .

"Let *go,*" Theodore whined, and I realized that *I* was holding *his* hand too tight.

"Sorry," I said, and to make up for it, I played spider fingers on his arm and sang his favorite song about eating worms.

Velma looked at us and sighed, shaking her head. Mr. Katz told a joke about a dentist. Then he told another one about two women in a butcher shop. All the grownups laughed and Mrs. Katz laughed the loudest and the longest.

Then the all-clear siren began to blow and we all stood and smiled at one another. Daddy began to lead us upstairs again. Velma was still grumbling about her beauty mask and about being interrupted.

Daddy tucked his arm in hers. "Be grateful," he said, "that it's only an air-raid *drill,* and not the real thing." Some of the grownups murmured in agreement as we climbed the stairs.

"What has forty eyes, green wings, and a bad disposition?" Mr. Katz called out.

"What has?" Mrs. Katz said, but then a door slammed shut and I never heard the answer.

two

Poor Theodore

The next day I came out of school and saw Theodore waiting, as usual, to walk home with me. His feet shuffled in my outgrown galoshes and his nose was running. My heart swelled with love for him, and I squeezed his mittened hand when we crossed the street until he shrieked with pain.

Poor Theodore, he had so many problems. Right from the beginning, people said terrible things about him. "I never saw such a sour baby," Aunt Lena said. "His face could stop an eight-day clock," the rich great-uncle added, rattling the change in his pockets.

It was true that Theodore was different from other kids. Everything he did seemed to be a little harder for him than for anyone else. When he cut his first tooth, he screamed all night. When he had the chicken pox, he was sicker than any other kid in the neighborhood. When he first learned to walk, his feet turned in and he fell all the time. Once he fell against a glass-topped coffee table and he had to have stitches in *three* different places. I remember best the sound of his crying, a sort of whoop, whoop, whoop, like the noise of the air-raid siren.

When Theodore began to speak, he stuttered, and when he was six years old he broke his first permanent tooth by falling off his chair during supper. Poor Theodore. He seemed to be visited by the meanest fairy in the kingdom, just like Sleeping Beauty. I decided to be Theodore's good witch. Somehow I would help him to change. I would help him with his schoolwork and he would become a real scholar. His name would be on the Honor Roll and he would be the teacher's pet. I made a secret vow that he would live at least until his Bar Mitzvah, and since he had already suffered two concussions and a case of double pneumonia, his chances didn't look that good. To protect him, I had to be his close companion. Being close, I fell in love with him.

I didn't even waste the time we spent walking home from school. Instead, I drilled him in spelling and arithmetic. "Two and two?" I asked. "How much is two and two?"

His fingers moved inside the mitten. "F-four?" he answered, and I kissed the sleeve of his plaid jacket.

"Four and four?"

Just then two nuns turned the corner and came toward us. The wind came gustily at the same moment and I think to Theodore *they* were the wind, or some terrible swooping black birds, their robes whipping out like wings.

Theodore pinched my finger. "D-do they like people?" he whispered.

"Of course," I told him. "Of course. Can't you see? They're people *themselves*."

But when they passed us he shuddered, and when they reached the corner behind us he turned, dragging his feet to watch until they were out of sight. "D-do they l-like boys?"

"Oh, for heaven's sakes!" I cried. "Don't tell me you're going to be a little sissy!" As soon as I said it, I was sorry. Without thinking, I had joined the enemy. It was true that Theodore was scared of just about everything. But if *I* didn't pretend he was a strong brave boy, nobody else ever would. I was his last chance.

When we got home—after running past the basement

entrance, of course—I tried to make it up to him. I un-buttoned his jacket and pulled off his mittens although he was certainly old enough to do all that himself. I rolled my eyes and sang crazy instant songs for him in a very high-pitched voice. "Oh Theodore, leave your galoshes on the floor, you are the one that I adore, forever mo-ore!" I tap-danced wildly on the little space of wooden floor at the edge of the living-room rug.

Velma kept turning around at the desk where she was doing her homework. She shook her head and gave us dirty looks, but I didn't pay any attention to her.

During supper I tickled his leg under the table and he choked on his mashed potatoes. Mother had to pound him on the back. "Enough!" she said. "Stop it right now!" as if he was choking on purpose.

"Infants," Velma said, sniffing. She's three years older than me and she was going to the big high school. It seemed that Velma and I hardly talked to one another except to say "Don't touch my things" or "Lower that radio," or something else that would start an argument.

Daddy just smiled at us, his eyeglasses all steamed up from the hot food. It was hard to make *him* angry, unless you did something to harm the war effort. He always tried to help Theodore too, by being very patient with him and by calling him Ted and Sport and other manly names. He called me Shirley-girl.

After dinner Velma and my mother washed the dishes and my father went inside to lie down on the sofa and read the evening paper. We could hear him clucking his tongue and sighing over the war news. Then he fell asleep and I took the opened newspaper right out of his hands without waking him up. My father worked in a factory where ladies' dresses were made. He was a cutter, which meant that he had to cut pieces of fabric with a very sharp-bladed machine, in exact sizes and shapes, following a paper pattern. Later, sewing-machine operators put the pieces together and they became dresses that were sold in big department stores. My father's trousers always had a rainbow of colored threads all over them. That night, while he slept on the sofa, Theodore and I pulled the threads off, very carefully one at a time, and rolled them into a beautiful thread ball. At eight o'clock Mother called, "Theodore! Bedtime!" and he followed me into the room the two of us shared. Velma had the other, very tiny bedroom all to herself, and our parents slept on a high-riser bed in the living room. Every night it had to be opened before they went to sleep, and every morning my father closed it again before he went to work. My mother said that someday Theodore would have the little bedroom and Velma and I would share the bigger one. As soon as Theodore was a little older. As soon as he was a little less afraid of everything.

Now he took his pajamas from the bureau drawer and went into the bathroom to brush his teeth, while I got the room ready for him. I plumped his pillow and turned down the covers. Then I took the rubber plant off the top of the bureau because at night its shadow looked exactly like an octopus. Of course I couldn't take away his memory of the octopus. He shivered under the quilt. I looked under his bed and in the closet. "Nobody here and nobody here," I said. "All clear. Safe and sound. Good night. Sweet dreams." I patted the nervous lump that was Theodore and tiptoed out of the room.

three

Being Thankful

In the morning, when Theodore and I were leaving for school, we met Mrs. Golub, who lived by herself in apartment 3H. She was the only grownup I knew who kept scrapbooks of movie stars. My mother always said that Mrs. Golub was star-struck, and when she said it she shook her head to let us know that Mrs. Golub was someone to feel sorry for, like an orphan. Poor foolish Mrs. Golub. She lived all alone and it was said that she talked to herself when there was no one else to listen.

That morning Mrs. Golub was waiting for us just outside the building, her breath blowing out in little white
clouds. "Hello, Shirley," she said, falling right into step
with us. "And how is the little fellow doing this morning?" But she never waited for an answer. "I saw Clark
in that new movie at the Loew's," she said. "What a man!
So handsome! So debonair!"

Clark was Clark Gable, the famous actor. Actors and
actresses were all Mrs. Golub ever talked about. And she
talked about them as if she knew them personally, as if
they were her very best friends, calling them Joan and
Clark and Barbara. "No wonder all those Hollywood
marriages end up in divorce," Mrs. Golub said, walking
along beside us. "I'd like to see what Mrs. Average House-
wife would do if she had to put up with all the pressures
of the Silver Screen. All that kissing and hugging they
have to do, for the cameras. They just want to be treated
like ordinary human beings, but people don't give them a
chance. Take Bette, for instance, or Joan. I just love Joan.
She is really a sincere person."

"Mrs. Golub," I said, interrupting her. "Don't you
think Theodore is handsome?"

She frowned as if she couldn't understand what I'd said,
as if I had awakened her from a very deep sleep. I suppose
she was dreaming of herself walking on Sunset Boulevard
in Hollywood, wearing beautiful flowered beach pajamas.

I had pulled her back to the slushy Brooklyn street. She touched her tight henna-red curls with one hand and tugged on the fox collar of her coat with the other. "What's that, sweetheart?" she asked.

It seemed useless but I went on anyway, for Theodore's sake. "I said, don't you think my brother is handsome?"

She bent down and pulled the cap back from Theodore's forehead. He was always very pale in the winter and his eyes and hair were pale as well. He looked back at her like a sleepy rabbit. He snuffled and blinked.

"Mmmmmm," she said, and then she put one gloved finger on Theodore's nose. "Do you see that?" she asked, and I wondered if something terrible had grown there since I'd looked at him last. Theodore wriggled. "Hold still, sweetie," Mrs. Golub ordered. "Look, hon, do you see that bridge there? It wouldn't make it. It just wouldn't photograph. God knows, a thing like that could make you or break you in Hollywood. Between you and me, I heard that John had to have his remade before they'd even touch him."

I sighed. I wasn't the least bit interested in turning Theodore into a movie star. I was just hoping that Mrs. Golub would say something *nice* about him to give him some self-confidence. But it was no use. If the subject wasn't movie stars and Hollywood, Mrs. Golub simply wasn't interested. I was glad when we got to school and she said goodbye to us. "Ta ta, kiddies," she said, waving her fingers, and turned and headed back toward home.

Theodore and I entered the schoolyard, where the lines were already forming for the different grades. Theodore shuffled over to the first-grade line and I joined my best friend, Mitzi Bloom, who was standing with the other sixth-graders.

Mitzi and I were opposites. She was tall and slender and she had fine blond hair, and I was short and a little plump and my head was a mess of dark curls. We had been best friends since the first grade. Sometimes we had terrible fights and wouldn't talk to each other for days, but we couldn't stay angry forever. For one thing, Mitzi told wonderful jokes and almost any time you looked at her she was smiling or making crazy faces or doing something goofy that made you laugh.

For another thing, I was always on the Honor Roll at school, ever since the first grade, and Mitzi didn't do too well in arithmetic and spelling, even though she was very smart. So we really needed each other.

"Knock knock," she said, as I approached the sixth-grade line.

"Who's there?"

"Ida."

"Ida who?"

"Ida wanna go to school!"

"Ha ha," I said. "Me too." Which wasn't really true. I liked school, even though I would never admit it to anyone. I even liked the school smells, the chalk, the musty smell of the clothes closet, the paper and ink smells of the books when I opened them on my desk. We had a sunny, cheerful room that year. Our teacher, Miss Cohen, had plants all over the place, and pictures hanging on every wall. There were signs about the war effort too. A SLIP OF THE LIPS SINKS SHIPS, said one, which meant you were not supposed to repeat any information about U.S. troops, in case an enemy spy was listening. Sometimes when Mitzi looked at the signs she would get a strange sad expression on her face and I knew she was thinking about her brother, Buddy, who was in the Army somewhere in Germany. He was only eighteen years old but he had joined the Army the day after his birthday. Sometimes they didn't get a letter from him for weeks, and the whole Bloom family would worry and wait downstairs in the hallway of their building for the mailman to come.

Mitzi's mother hung a little silk flag in the window, with a single blue star on it. That meant there was a serviceman in the family. A flag with two blue stars meant that there were two servicemen, but one with a gold star on it meant that the serviceman in that family had been killed in the war. There were none like that in the windows of our building, although there were about eight of them with blue stars.

Mitzi was happy today. There had been a letter from Buddy the day before and he said that he was fine and they were not to worry about him. But worrying was all the Blooms seemed to know how to do. When Mitzi and I went to a war movie at the Loew's theater, she clutched my hand every time a gun was fired or a bomb exploded, and I knew she was thinking about Buddy.

I never told Mitzi, but I thought about Buddy a lot, too. In fact, I'd had a secret crush on him ever since I was in the fourth grade and he nicknamed me Peewee. No one else ever called me that, and when Buddy did, I pretended I didn't like it at all.

Now I wrote my real name in the top left-hand corner of a folded sheet of yellow paper. We were going to have a spelling test and I wrote Miss Cohen's name in the right-hand corner and the date right under it. November 15, 1944.

The spelling words were lovely, long and full of tricky sounds. I loved to spell and I never got less than 100 on a spelling test. Someday I was going to enter the National Spelling Bee. Last year we read in the newspaper about a boy in East Bridgewater, Massachusetts, who had beaten a girl from Grand Ledge, Michigan, on the word "iridescent."

Miss Cohen read the words aloud to us, saying them very clearly and carefully. I knew she felt the same way about words that I did. She was always saying that reading was an adventure and that books were a magic carpet that could take you anywhere you wanted to go, and other things like that. I looked up from my paper after the third word and saw that she was staring dreamily through the window at the gray winter sky. I suppose she was thinking about her boyfriend, who was a sailor on a Navy ship somewhere in the Pacific Ocean.

After the spelling test, we went to the auditorium for an assembly. Another sixth-grade class was going to present a play called *The Pilgrim's Dream,* which was written by Mrs. Whitman, their teacher, and some of my friends were going to be in it.

Half of the kids were Pilgrims and they wore big white paper collars. The lucky ones got to be Indians, though, with gorgeous feathers and lots of makeup. The play started with the Pilgrims all worried about how they were going to survive the terrible winter in America. One of the Pilgrim fathers kept waving to his friends in the audience and smiling while he said his lines about the harsh weather and all the hardships his people had suffered. There was a lot of other stuff about the Indians and how they managed to live with nature and get along.

Then one Pilgrim had a dream. In his dream a long

table was set with wonderful food and drink. Everyone was happy, singing and smiling. The Indians kept coming to the door bringing presents, including a large cardboard turkey that was supposed to be alive and struggling to get free.

When the Pilgrim woke up, yawning and stretching, he had to rub his eyes because his dream had come true. That same cardboard turkey was supposed to be cooked and stuffed and it was sitting in the middle of the table. "Oh, we thank thee," the Pilgrim said, looking up.

Then all the other Pilgrims came onstage, and a couple of the Indians did too. They all joined hands, facing the audience, and began to sing "We gather together to ask the Lord's blessing."

I wondered how the Indians were supposed to know the words to that song, but as they sang and Mrs. Whitman played the piano, crossing her arms and crashing her fingers down on the keys, a wonderful feeling came over me. Suddenly I felt thankful too. I was glad to be me, in P.S. 247 in Brooklyn, New York, sitting next to my best friend. I believed that the Allies were going to win the war, that Buddy would surely come home again and we would have a big wonderful party for him. I thought of my mother and father and Theodore and even my sister, Velma, and how much I loved them. Tears came to my eyes, but I felt happier than I ever had before in my life. The play was over. The Pilgrims and the Indians kept bowing and everyone applauded, even though two of the Pilgrims were caught on the wrong side when the curtain came down.

four
Grandpa Small

On Sunday I didn't feel very happy at all. It was my turn to go with my father and mother to visit Grandpa Small in the old-age home. He had been there a long time, ever since Grandma Small died, when I was little. I couldn't even remember her. Grandpa Small was old and very sick. One of his big problems was his memory. He couldn't remember things that had happened five minutes before, but sometimes he remembered things that had happened thirty or forty years ago.

I didn't know why I had to go at all. He hardly ever remembered who I was. He'd call me Etta sometimes, which is my mother's name, or Rifka, who was his wife, my Grandmother Small. Aunt Lena and Aunt Millie shouted at him, because he was deaf, "Papa, this is *Shirley*. You know—Etta's girl!" He only smiled, looking absent-minded, like someone who couldn't find his eyeglasses. Then two minutes later he called me Lena or Millie or Rifka again.

We had to take a subway train and then a trolley car to get to the old-age home, which was on the other side of Brooklyn. All the way there I'd keep thinking about how lucky Theodore was because everybody said he was too young to visit Grandpa Small. Twice a month I stayed home with him and Velma went. Twice a month she was Theodore's baby-sitter and I went with my parents. It was my turn again this cold and windy November day. I looked back up at our kitchen window and I could see Theodore's face pressed against the glass. Lucky stiff, I thought. He didn't have to go to that awful place where everyone was so old and sick.

As soon as you walked into the old-age home there was a funny smell, sour and stale. It was much too hot and you could hear the steam bubbling in all the radiators. There were always lots of other visitors there on Sunday. Whole families came, some on the trolley car with us, others by automobile. They brought packages, big shopping bags filled with food and plants and warm socks. Some of the old people waited in wheelchairs in a big room called the solarium. Grandpa Small used to be in the solarium when we came, but this time he was lying in bed propped up on three pillows. Aunt Lena and Aunt Millie were already there when we arrived. "Look who's here, Papa!" Aunt Lena cried. "It's Etta and Morris and Shirley!"

The smell in Grandpa Small's room was even worse than the one in the hallway. There were two beds in the room, the kind with a handle in the front that you could turn to crank the mattress up or down. There was a man in the other bed and he seemed to be fast asleep. His face was terribly yellow and his skin looked as if it were made of crumpled tissue paper. A woman sat on the visitor's chair next to his bed reading a book. I wondered if the old man even knew she was there.

My mother pushed me gently ahead of her. "Say hello," she whispered, just as if I were a little baby who didn't know what to do.

"Hello, Grandpa," I said, and for some reason I remembered the story of Little Red Riding Hood. Grandpa, what big ears you have, I thought, but of course I didn't say it. Instead, I leaned close, shutting my eyes and holding my breath at the same time, and put a very fast kiss on my grandfather's cheek. He reached out then and patted my hand. Everybody acted as if something wonderful had happened, but I felt a little sad.

"You see?" Aunt Lena said. "Do you see how happy he is to see you?"

"Shirley brought you some prunes, Papa," my mother said, reaching into her shopping bag. Of course that wasn't true. My mother had brought the prunes herself. She had even cooked them that morning before we left the house. I didn't say anything about it, though. I just stayed in a corner, trying to make myself very small so that they would all forget about me until it was time to go home.

The door was open and I could see people wheeling some of the old women and men past in their wheelchairs. Everybody talked very loud and in cheerful voices. I could hear people saying, "Isn't that nice, Mama?" "Isn't that beautiful, Uncle Willie?" "Aren't you glad, Papa?" I wondered why everyone was so phony, making believe that all those poor sick people were happy. I made up my mind then and there that when I was old I would never be like Grandpa Small, who couldn't even remember his own children's names. I didn't know exactly how I would do it, but I was going to be a strong old lady who could do anything, even jump rope or ride a bicycle if I wanted to, and who could remember everyone I ever met in my whole life.

I was glad when the nurses and attendants started coming into the rooms saying, "Visiting's over now. Time to go home, folks." A big fat woman with a very red nose looked into Grandpa Small's room. "How's my boyfriend?" she asked, winking at me. "Time to go, folks."

This time it was my father who pushed me forward to say goodbye.

"Goodbye, Grandpa," I said, kissing his other cheek. "Rifka?" he asked.

My mother and father looked at each other across the bed and my mother lowered her eyes. Then she squeezed Grandpa's hand. "It's me, Papa. It's Etta. I'm going home now. Take care, Papa."

The woman visiting the other old man put a card in her book to mark her place and tiptoed out of the room.

I was surprised to see how dark it was when we went outside again. I walked between my mother and father to the trolley station, holding their hands. My father kept swinging our arms forward and back. The air smelled so sweet and fresh and cold. I started to skip and my father laughed, skipping along with me, but Mother pulled back. "Stop it," she said. "Morris, sometimes you're like a big baby! Watch out! I'm going to lose my shoe!" But she was smiling and she didn't sound angry at all.

Later, sitting in the subway train, she started talking about Grandpa Small when he was a young man. "You can't imagine," she said, "how handsome he was. Very tall and he had lots of thick dark hair. I think you inherited yours from him, Shirley."

I tried to picture Grandpa Small as a young man with thick hair, but it was impossible. All I could think of was the thin, bald old man propped up like a baby on three pillows.

"When I was very little," my mother continued, "he took me ice skating in the park. We went at night when the moon lit up the whole world. We wore long, long red scarves that my mother knitted for us."

The subway train raced through a tunnel and my mother smiled to herself, remembering.

I leaned against my father's shoulder thinking of all the people I knew. I thought there were about a million of them, but I remembered everyone's name. I started with the children in my class. Mitzi, I thought. Renee and Jeanette and Sylvia and Martin and Gloria. Morty, I thought, and Sammy and Ruth and Elliot. Paul. Steven. Elaine. Muriel. My head banged gently against my father's shoulder with the motion of the train.

five

Cure No. 1:
The Ghost in the Closet

Mitzi and I were training Theodore to be scare-proof. It was really Mitzi's idea in the first place. If we could get him used to being scared, she said, it would be harder and harder to scare him. Eventually he would be brave. We made Theodore sit in a chair in the living room with his back to the doorway.

Velma was in her little room listening to the radio and my mother was in the kitchen making dinner.

"Now don't turn around, Theodore," Mitzi warned.

"Just keep sitting there."

"What are you going to do?" I whispered.

Mitzi made a werewolf face at me, holding up her hands like claws.

"Oh, don't," I said. "He'll drop dead. He's scared of his own shadow already."

Mitzi thought about it. "Okay. We'll start slowly. We'll just make scary sounds for a while." She motioned for me to hide just outside the doorway with her. Then she put her finger to her lips. "Theodooore Braaavermaaan," she said, in a very spooky voice.

"Wh-what?" Theodore asked.

"This is a ghooooost speeeeaking."

"I d-don't like g-ghosts," Theodore said. He started to get out of the chair.

"Siiiiit doooown," Mitzi said, "or I'm going to get yoooooou."

"Listen," I said. "Maybe . . ."

Mitzi squeezed my shoulder. "It's for his own good," she reminded me. "Just be quiet." Then she leaned her face toward the living room again. "Theodooooore."

"W-what do you w-want?"

"You must do a very brave deed, Theo-dooore."

"I h-have to go to the bathroom," Theodore said.

"Noooo, you dooon't. You have to do a very brave deed."

"What are you going to make him do?" I whispered.

"I don't know," Mitzi said cheerfully. "I'll think of

something." Then she giggled, and I felt like giggling too, in the dark hallway, even though I was a little worried about Theodore. What if he fainted?

"I've *got* it," Mitzi said then. She moved her arms wildly, motioning for me to go into the hall closet.

"I *can't*," I said.

But Mitzi just kept waving her arms. "Do you want him to be the biggest sissy in America?" she hissed at me.

"No-o," I said, moving slowly toward the closet.

"Get in," she said. "Hurry up."

With a last look at Theodore's chair in the living room, I ran to the hall closet and went inside. It was jam-packed with winter coats and there was hardly any room for me. I left the door open a tiny crack for light and air.

Mitzi called in to Theodore again. "Here is the brave deed you have to do," she said.

"I have to do my homework," Theodore said.

"Later," Mitzi told him.

I wished she would just tell him what to do and get it over with. It was awfully stuffy in the closet, and all those woolen coats made my nose itch.

"Go to the hall cloooset," Mitzi moaned. "Open the door and let my little ghost sister free."

"I-I have three n-numbers to write," Theodore said. "I-I *have* to do my h-homework." He sounded as if he was going to cry.

I could hear my mother singing in the kitchen as she

beat something with an egg beater.

"If you do not let my little sister freeeee," Mitzi said, "she will come back to haunt yooooou."

Theodore was making funny little sniffling sounds. I was beginning to be sorry we started the whole thing. What did Mitzi expect me to do anyway? I opened the door a little wider. "Psst," I said. "I can't stay here all day. What am I supposed to do in this stupid closet?"

"Scare him," she said. "When he opens the door, you just scream Boo! at him. That should do it. I bet it will cure him. I bet he'll never be scared again in his whole life."

I felt very doubtful. Did you cure pneumonia by putting somebody in ice water? Could you cure a sissy by scaring him half to death?

"I don't know . . ." I said, but Mitzi ran over and slammed the door right in my face. It was pitch black in the closet. I wondered how much oxygen there was in there, anyway. What if I died of suffocation and Theodore opened the door and a corpse fell out? Then Mitzi would be sorry. I couldn't see anything and it was difficult to hear what was going on outside. I pressed my ear against the door and listened.

"Just keep your eyes shut, Theodore," Mitzi was saying, "until I tell you to open them."

I couldn't hear any sound from Theodore at all, but

Mitzi's voice got louder, as if she was coming closer to the closet.

"Go ahead," she said. "Open your eyes now. Then open the closet door and let my little ghost sister's spirit free or she will haunt you every night!"

Poor Theodore. He must have been scared out of his wits. The whole thing was stupid. It just wouldn't work. We would have to wait until he "grew out of it," as my mother said.

I could hear something then. Someone was turning the doorknob to open the closet door. Mitzi was crazy if she thought I was going to say Boo! and scare my own little brother silly. I gripped the other side of the door handle. As soon as Theodore opened the door I was going to tell him to forget the whole thing. *If* he opened it before my oxygen ran out. I leaned against the door then and it opened suddenly, and I fell right out, practically into Theodore's arms. "See!" I said. "It's only me!" I smiled brightly at him, but Theodore had looked at me as if I really were a ghost and then he ran shrieking down the hallway. He screamed louder than he ever had before. Mitzi put her hands over her ears and shut her eyes, but I ran after Theodore. "It was only a joke!" I said. "Look, Theodore, it's only Shirley. It's only me!"

But he just went crashing ahead, still screaming, until he collided with the door at the other end of the hall.

Mother came out of the kitchen with the egg beater still in her hand. "What on earth . . .?"

Velma came running out of her room, too. The woman who lived in the apartment underneath us began banging on her ceiling with a broom, which she did every time we made too much noise.

Theodore had gone into the door with his head, butting it just like an old goat. He had a big bump on his forehead and it was turning blue.

"What happened?" Mother said, over and over again.

Theodore had his mouth opened wide but no sound came out at all. He just kept pointing his finger at me.

"Did you hit him in the head?" Velma asked.

"I didn't . . ." I said. "I didn't do . . . I only wanted . . ."

It was no use trying to explain. Theodore had his voice back again and he sounded more like the air-raid siren than ever.

Mitzi grabbed her coat and ran to the door. She looked back at me as if to say she was sorry and then she was gone.

I went to the refrigerator for a piece of ice to put on Theodore's forehead, but he wouldn't talk to me.

I wrapped the ice in a washcloth and held it gently against his head. "The-o-dore," I sang, in a very quiet voice. "I won't do that any-more."

He didn't forgive me until after supper. And he

wasn't cured at all. If anything, he was worse than ever. He wouldn't go to sleep without a light on.

I remembered the terrible darkness in the closet and Mitzi's ghost voice floating toward me, and I really didn't mind the night light myself.

six

Miss Cohen's Announcement

Walking to school with Theodore the next day, I promised myself that I'd never talk to Mitzi Bloom again. It was all her fault that I got into so much trouble the night before. It was all her fault that Theodore had an egg-shaped blue and yellow lump on his forehead that morning.

When she smiled at me on the sixth-grade line, I just turned my head away and looked across the schoolyard, where the kindergarten babies were lined up, holding hands. I had gone to kindergarten in the same school. Had I ever been that little? It didn't seem possible. Yet I remembered the big kindergarten room with its doll corner, a place where I was the mother of some naked and raggedy doll. I remembered rest time, lying in a little patch of sunlight on my yellow blanket and thinking dream thoughts, even though I was still awake.

Mitzi kept hissing at me and saying "Shir-*ley,*" but I pretended I couldn't hear her at all. She wasn't going to get *me* into trouble ever again.

Finally the bell rang and we all walked into the building and went to our classrooms. Miss Cohen was waiting at her desk. Just before the pledge to the flag, Mitzi leaned over and said, "Are you *mad* at me or something?" As if she didn't know. Then it was time to stand and I didn't answer her.

After the pledge, Morty Levine, the boy sitting at the next desk, passed a folded piece of paper to me. I looked at him, raising my eyebrows, but he shrugged his shoulders and pointed to Mitzi.

I opened the note. It said, "Roses are red, violets are blue, if you won't be glad, I'll go live in the zoo!" There was a tiny drawing of a monkey wearing a dress just like Mitzi's. Of course I had to smile. I couldn't help it. The monkey looked so funny and cute. How could I be mad at Mitzi for very long? I turned around and smiled at her and she smiled back, and then she made a monkey face at me and I laughed out loud.

Miss Cohen tapped on her desk with a ruler. "If you're ready, young ladies," she said, and I turned around to face her. "Now," Miss Cohen continued, "I have an announcement to make. There is going to be an interborough competition in spelling." A few of the boys groaned and Miss Cohen tapped the ruler again.

I sat up very straight in my seat to listen, forgetting about Mitzi and the monkey note. A spelling competition!

"For those of you who are interested," Miss Cohen said, "there will be a preliminary spelling bee in Dr. Vanderbilt's office in a few weeks. It will be held at three o'clock, just after school ends for the day. The winner will go on to compete with winners from other schools in our district. The district winner will compete to determine the best speller in Brooklyn. Finally there will be a bee to name the best speller in all the public elementary schools in the City of New York. The grand winner will receive a gold medal and a special citation from the mayor."

The best speller in New York City! I began to think of all the big words I could spell. Institution, I thought. Representation. Receive, committee, hospitality, government. The best speller in all of New York City. Would it end there? Who knows? I began to think about it. The best speller in New York State. The best speller in the

United States of America. Ladies and gentlemen, introducing Shirley Braverman, the greatest little speller in the
world!

". . . and you may pick up your application blanks at
my desk on your way home this afternoon," Miss Cohen
was saying. "Remember, you must have your parents'
permission to enter the spelling competition, so be sure
one of them signs in the right place."

I came back to the classroom again, a little ashamed of
my daydreaming. After all, I didn't know that I was the
best speller, did I? Then I thought of all my test papers,
marked A+, 100, Excellent. I hadn't missed a word all
year, even the ones that Miss Cohen called "challenging."
At home, Velma, and even Mother, would ask me how to
spell something once in a while.

I took a piece of paper from my notebook and wrote,
"Roses are red, violets are blue. Confidentially speaking,
I'm not mad at you." I asked Morty to pass the note to
Mitzi. Confidentially. That was another hard word. I
wondered how the gold medal would look on my blue
winter coat.

seven

Before and After

"The trouble with Theodore," Mitzi said, "is that he doesn't have big muscles. You never see anyone picking on Popeye the way they pick on Theodore, do you?"

We were on our way home from school, with Theodore walking a few feet behind us. He kept turning around every few minutes to see if we were being followed. There was a much older boy who had been picking on Theodore and scaring him half to death. Mitzi and I looked for him in the schoolyard. If we found him we were going to tell him to stop being such a big bully, but he was nowhere in sight.

"My mother and father don't want Theodore to fight," I said.

"He doesn't have to," Mitzi explained. "If he looks tough, if he has big muscles, nobody will ever start up with him in the first place. That bully only picks on him because he's such a puny little kid."

I turned around and looked at Theodore and I had to admit that Mitzi was right. He looked very little walking all by himself, and he *was* pretty skinny and pale besides.

"The thing is," Mitzi said, "we have to help him build up his muscles. I'll come over later and show you something."

We parted at the next corner and I waited for Theodore to catch up. "What did that boy say to you again?" I asked him.

"H-he said he was going to g-give me an Indian burn, and he said he was going to get me into trouble, i-if I didn't give h-him my baseball cards and my m-marbles."

"That big bully! I bet he wouldn't pick on someone his own size! Don't worry, Theodore. I won't let him hurt you."

But Theodore looked worried anyway. He was still watching for that bully over his shoulder when we entered the lobby of our apartment house.

When Mitzi came over later, she had a big stack of her favorite comic books with her. She handed a pile of them to each of us. "Here. Look through these. We want to find the ads for body-building."

"What?" Theodore said.

"Theodore, don't worry," Mitzi said. "Leave it to us. Just look for an ad with a picture of a man with great big bulging muscles."

Theodore started turning the pages and in a few minutes he forgot all about the ad because he was so busy looking at the comics.

But Mitzi and I looked very carefully. We read the ads for little machines that pull blackheads right out of your skin, and the ones for marvelous magic tricks that could "fool your friends and amaze your relatives!" There was one ad for a special brassiere that was supposed to help girls with small busts look glamorous. The ads were really much more interesting than the comics.

Finally Mitzi said, "Here it is! This is the one we want. Listen to this, Shirley. 'We can build you a better body in just thirty days or your money back! King Sandor was once like you, afraid to stand up for his rights, afraid of threatening bullies who tried to take his girl and his job away. King Sandor was once a skinny helpless weakling! When you look at his picture, this will be hard for you to believe, but through his special, scientifically devised, secret muscle-building plan, King Sandor became the he-man he is today. Send for our *free* instruction booklet that will come to you in a plain brown envelope, without cost or obligation. Don't delay and we will include a beautiful free portrait of King Sandor, suitable for framing.' "

Mitzi turned the book around so that I could look at King Sandor's pictures, Before and After. In the Before picture, King Sandor looked even skinnier than Theodore. He was wearing loose-fitting swim trunks and he was standing on the beach with very poor posture and a sad expression on his face.

But in the After picture, which almost filled the rest of the page, King Sandor had muscles as big as watermelons. He was wearing tight leopard-skin trunks and leather wristbands and a great big smile. He didn't look anything like the King Sandor in the Before picture. "Wow!" I said. It *was* hard to believe. I read the ad myself. It said, "Without cost or obligation" in plain English. "Okay," I told Mitzi. "Let's do it!"

We decided to send for the instruction booklet under the name of S. Braverman at my address. I was the only S. Braverman in the family and King Sandor had no way of knowing that I was a girl. Even while we were filling out the coupon, Theodore just sat there looking at Superman and Blondie and Nancy and Sluggo, as if he didn't have a care in the world.

Mitzi licked the envelope and sealed it shut. "Make a muscle, Theodore," she said.

He turned the page of the comic book and held his arm out without looking up. It looked as straight and skinny as a pencil.

Mitzi squeezed it. "Mush!" she said. "But we'll take care of *that!*"

We shook hands on it over Theodore's head.

eight
Style 482

On Saturday my father took me to the dress factory with him. There had been a big shipment of fabric on Friday and he had to go in on the weekend to help his boss, Mr. Hamberger, get it ready. He took me along for company.

My father and I rode the subway to the factory. I brought my book *Words That Stump the Experts* along so I could study my spelling during the train ride. Daddy wiped his eyeglasses clean and he opened the book on his lap as the train left the station. "Okay, Shirley-girl," he said. "How about 'exaggerate'?"

I spelled it for him, loving the way his eyes opened wide when I did it correctly.

He patted my head. "With a good brain and a good education," he said, "you can do anything you want in this life."

I knew it was his dream to send all three of us to college, even though he and Mother never had a chance to go themselves. "Give me another word," I said, feeling very proud.

" 'Fascination,' " he said, and the train rumbled on, taking us to Avenue U, where the dress factory was.

Mr. Hamberger was a fat man, but he never looked jolly. He always seemed aggravated. He pinched my cheek, but he really wasn't paying any attention to me. Then he started complaining. "Morris," he said, "it's a good thing you're here. Yesterday that truckman was late. Today I see a whole bundle is ruined with water stains." Mr. Hamberger kept pulling on the few hairs left on his head.

The factory wasn't as busy on Saturday as it was during the week, but there were still some people working overtime. Three operators, their sewing machines singing, their feet pumping the pedals, waved to me and blew kisses. The presser, Dominick, smiled through the steam of his pressing board at me. His shirt was open at the neck and his sleeves were rolled up.

My father patted Mr. Hamberger on the back. "Don't worry," he said, but Mr. Hamberger kept complaining. "Today, Operator No. 3 has a bellyache. Operator No. 4 has a kid with the measles. Why didn't I go into the printing business with my brother Lou?"

"Don't worry, Mr. H.," my father said again. "Stop worrying. Everything will be all right."

My father put his apron on and went to the big cutting table, where a large sheet of paper was laid out. He placed the pattern pieces on the paper and traced their outlines with black chalk. Then he put the patterns aside and took the paper off the table as well. He unrolled a huge bolt of material in many layers across the table and put the paper with the black outlines on top. Each shape on the paper represented a different part of a dress: a sleeve, a collar, a skirt. After laying heavy weights across the paper, he began to cut the pieces out with an electric cutting machine.

One of the operators gave me a bunch of yellow tickets that said Style 482, Size 14, and she showed me how to thread the tickets through the belt loops on the dresses. It was fun. I pretended that I was all grown and that this was my real job. I named myself Finisher No. 23. In my imagination, Mr. Hamberger told my father that if it wasn't for Finisher No. 23, he'd have to close his shop.

"Look at those tickets," Mr. H. said, inside my head. "Perfect! What a job!"

Behind me, the operators tried to sing louder than their machines, the presser whistled like a bird, and my father's electric cutter knifed through the fabric.

Just when I began to get tired, when the color yellow seemed like the worst color in the world, Operator No. 16 came back and gave me a new rack of dresses and a new bunch of tickets, green ones this time, marked Style 482, Size 12. She smiled at me and went back to her sewing machine.

I did all the green tickets and then all the blue ones marked Size 10 and then I realized that something strange had happened. All the noises in the shop had died down, almost at once. The machines were quiet, the presser's steam had stopped hissing. My father was rerolling a bolt of cloth and then stacking it in a bin with other bolts.

I rubbed my eyes and wriggled my fingers. They felt stiff and tired.

"Well, Shirley-girl," my father said. "Did you have a long enough working day? Are you ready to go home?"

Before I could answer, Mr. Hamberger came over to the cutting table. He polished a silver dollar against the side of his trousers and then he handed it to me. "You're a nice little girl," he said. "But don't marry anyone in the dress business. It's nothing but headaches."

"Don't worry, Mr. H.," my father said one more time, but Mr. Hamberger only shook his head sadly from side to side.

Just as we were leaving the factory, Operator No. 16, an old lady with gray hair pinned into a bun on top of her head, ran after us. "Wait, wait!" she called. "Morris, little girl, wait!"

I turned around and she handed a package to me. "It's a present," she said, and when I hesitated, "Go *ahead*. Take it, it's for you. I made it for you."

I opened the loosely wrapped package and found a tiny, perfect dress inside. Exactly like Style 482, only very, very small. I looked at it carefully and found a tiny hem and little buttonholes, just big enough for my smallest fingernail to pass through.

"Tell your dolly she should wear it in good health," said Operator No. 16. "And I hope it's a good fit!"

"Thank you," I said. "It's so— so perfect!" I didn't want to tell her that I had stopped playing with dolls almost a year ago. She looked so pleased that I couldn't hurt her feelings, and besides, I really did like the little dress for itself. I thought that when I got home I would make a tiny tag for it that said Style 482, Size 1.

Later, all alone in the bedroom, I took the dress out again and ran my finger over the miniature collar and cuffs. Just for the fun of it, I decided to look for my old dolls and see if it would fit one of them. In the doll box on the floor of the closet, I came across a little grownup doll, one with beautiful blond hair and high-heeled shoes. I remembered when I got her as a birthday present from Aunt Lena and Uncle Max. She came in a cardboard box that looked like a camp trunk, and she had a wedding gown and a pair of pajamas and an apron. Now she was naked, except for her shoes.

Mitzi and I played with her for hours almost every day. We called her Alice for a long time and then we renamed her Sonja, after Sonja Henie, the blond ice skater who was a movie actress as well.

Poor Sonja looked terrible now. She had been at the bottom of the doll box, under the heavy rubber baby doll and a very old one of Velma's with elbows and knees you could bend. "Poor little Sonja," I said, smoothing her hair and brushing some lint out of her blue eyes. "Don't worry. I have a beautiful new dress for you."

The dress was easy to put on because it had buttons all the way down the front, right to the hem. When the last one was closed, I saw that it *was* a perfect fit! It was as if Operator No. 16 had made the dress just for Sonja.

"Don't you look wonderful!" I said aloud. "Aren't you beautiful? This is Style 482, madam, our most popular number. Please look at the beautiful work, all these lovely stitches and everything. It fits like a dream, madam, and the color is very good for you." I held Sonja up to the dresser mirror and turned her around slowly, as if she were a model in a fashion show. "Do you see? This dress was made by our finest operator. Our best cutter cut out this material for you, and Finisher No. 23 did the finishing."

I looked in the mirror again and I saw Velma standing in the doorway staring at me. "What are you doing?" she said. "Are you playing with *dolls?*"

"Of course not," I said. "I don't play with stupid dolls any more. Somebody just gave me this stupid dress and I wanted to see if it fit, that's all."

Velma's eyes got very narrow. "Well, then who were you talking to?"

"Me? I wasn't talking to anybody." I threw Sonja behind me without even looking to see if she landed on the bed or not. There was a little thud and I guessed she'd fallen behind the bed. I wouldn't look, not when Velma was there, anyway. "I wasn't talking," I said. "I was *singing.*" Then, just to prove it, I began to sing at the top of my lungs. I never did have a very good voice. It always sort of cracked and squeaked when I tried a high note.

Pretty soon Velma went back to her own room.

As soon as she was gone, I knelt beside the bed and looked under it for Sonja. There she was, lying on her face next to one of my blue bedroom slippers. "Sorry, madam," I whispered, so that no one else could hear me. I smoothed her hair again and I fussed over her new dress. Then I put her back in the doll box and closed the closet door.

nine
"Hello, Ma?"

Theodore didn't improve much, in spite of my vows to help him. He wasn't on the Honor Roll for the first grade yet and people kept on calling him a sissy, and that big bully still picked on him. He fell down a whole flight of stairs in school one day and now he had another bump on the same side of his head. Poor Theodore.

I did feel a little guilty. I hadn't paid much attention to him lately. Ever since Miss Cohen had announced the spelling competition, I hardly thought of anything else.

Even during blackouts, I'd just sit in the dark and spell out big words inside my head. I think I wanted to win that competition more than anything else in the world.

Of course Mitzi wasn't going to enter it; she wasn't very good at spelling. But she was going to root for me. In fact, she was coaching me, too. On line in the schoolyard, and almost every afternoon after school, and even on some weekends, she helped me practice with *Words That Stump the Experts*. One day we were at my house working on Chapter 3, "Seven-Letter Words, Medium Hard," when Mitzi suddenly threw the book right down on the floor.

"Why did you do that?" I shrieked. I picked up the book and began to examine it for damage.

"Oh, nothing happened to your precious old book!" Mitzi said.

Luckily, it *was* unharmed, but Mitzi didn't even say she was sorry. In fact, she just jumped out of her chair and began to yell at me, as if *I* had done something to *her!* "I'm sick and tired of spelling, spelling, spelling! I'm sick and tired of that stupid spelling bee! We never do anything else any more. We never play Monopoly, we never play checkers, we never do anything!"

"You're just jealous!" I shouted back at her. "You're just plain mean and jealous!"

"Jealous? *Jealous?* I'm not jealous. I wouldn't want to enter that stupid spelling contest if you paid me. I have better things to do with my time!"

"Sour grapes! That's your trouble. You couldn't enter it if you wanted to."

"Oh, no?"

"No! It's not going to have easy words like c-a-t."

"I can spell *another* word that I wouldn't want to say out loud," Mitzi said.

"What? What?"

"I wouldn't want to call anyone in this room that word that *rhymes* with c-a-t."

"I don't even know what you're talking about," I said.

"I'm talking about r-a-t. With long whiskers and a mean little face."

"Are you calling me a *rat?*"

"I never said . . ."

"Oh, sticks and stones may break my bones . . ."

"R-A-T!"

"D-O-P-E!"

"Well, I'm going home, Shirley Braverman, and I'm never coming back again as long as I live."

"Good riddance to bad rubbish," I said, folding my arms.

Mitzi put her coat on so fast that she buttoned it all wrong and one side was longer than the other. She ran to the door and opened it. "R-A-T!" she shouted once more and this time her voice echoed all over the hallway.

"Sticks and stones . . ." I began again, but she had slammed the door hard.

I was so angry I couldn't even catch my breath. My eyes kept filling with tears and I wiped them away with my fists. I would never, ever talk to Mitzi Bloom again. To be jealous! To call your best friend a rat! She could pass a million notes to me in school. I would tear them all up. She could beg and plead. I was never going to talk to her again.

But if I was so angry, why was I crying? Old Mitzi Bloomers. Who needed her anyway? Who cared? She'd be sorry. She'd regret it when the mayor put that medal around my neck. Introducing Shirley Braverman, the best speller in the whole . . .

I began to sob and the tears spilled out faster than I could wipe them away. Finally I went into the bedroom and threw myself down on the bed so hard that the bedboards rattled. I cried and cried, getting my pillow all sloppy and wet, until I fell asleep.

Later, if my family noticed my red eyes and my sad face, they didn't mention it. Daddy had the radio on during supper. Even without trying to listen, I heard all the terrible words that had to do with war. Attack . . . bombing . . . killed . . . wounded . . . I wanted to tell them about my fight with Mitzi, but somehow I couldn't. I started thinking about the war. If best friends couldn't get along with one another, it was no wonder whole countries went to war. I sighed, hoping that somebody would ask me what was wrong, but nobody did.

Then Theodore spilled his milk and some of it ran off the table and down my leg. "You little baby!" I said to him. "Why don't you watch what you're doing?"

Theodore's eyes opened wide. Then he began to cry.

Oh, everything got worse and worse. I didn't mean to yell at him, but I wouldn't say that I was sorry, either. He didn't even know that I wasn't angry with him.

"I'm surprised at you, Shirley-girl," Daddy said, in a gentle voice.

I was surprised at myself, but I still didn't apologize.

After supper the doorbell rang and Velma went to see who it was. I heard her calling to Mother and saying, "Come in, come in," and then there was a jumble of voices in the hallway.

"What a nice surprise," I heard Mother say, her voice rising above the others. "Shirley, come say hello. Mitzi is here."

Mitzi! What was she doing in my house? She said she was never going to come back as long as she lived.

I walked slowly into the living room and Mitzi really was there, and so were her parents. Did they come over to talk to my parents about my fight with her?

Mitzi was sitting on the edge of the sofa, and she looked

as if she was ready to start running if anyone said boo to her. *Her* eyes were pretty red and swollen and she wouldn't look right at me.

"It's very nice of you, Mr. Braverman," Mr. Bloom said.

"Nice? Not at all. It's a pleasure," my father said. "And please let's not be formal. Call me Morris."

"Then you call me Sol," Mr. Bloom said.

"Would you like some coffee?" my mother asked.

It certainly didn't *sound* as if they came over to complain.

"Oh, thank you," Mitzi's mother said. "But we're so anxious to hear . . ."

"Of course," Mother answered. "Morris, warm up the machine. We'll have coffee later."

My father stood and walked to the phonograph. He pushed the switch and then he turned to Mr. Bloom. "It takes a few seconds to warm up," he said.

I was just going to ask what was going on when Mother told me and Theodore, who was standing shyly in the doorway. Buddy Bloom had made a recording of his own voice, with the Red Cross, near his battalion in Germany. The Red Cross had sent the record to the Blooms, but they didn't have a phonograph. Now we were all going to hear Buddy's voice.

My father tapped the point of the needle with his finger and there were loud popping noises. "Ahh," he said. "It's ready. The record?"

Mr. Bloom handed him a small black disc and everyone else was very, very still. Mrs. Bloom sat forward in her seat and she held one hand against her breast. My father lowered the needle to the record.

"Hello, Ma? Dad? This is Buddy."

There was a funny little noise from Mrs. Bloom, something like a laugh and a sob at the same time.

Buddy's voice continued. "Hi, Mitzi. How's my girl? Are you taking good care of Brooklyn for me? Say hello to your friend Peewee."

Peewee! That was me! Buddy remembered me!

"I'm doing fine," Buddy said, "so try not to worry about me." His voice *sounded* far away, a little scratchy and weak. "I miss you all a lot. I can't wait till this is all over and we can be together again. Ma, I keep thinking about your great cooking."

This time Mrs. Bloom really began to cry and Mr. Bloom put his arm around her.

"Well, I guess that's all the time I have now, folks," Buddy said. "Take good care of yourselves. I'll be seeing you soon."

And then there was just the sound of the phonograph needle going around and around in the last groove of the record. None of us moved. Mother had to say, "Shut it off, Morris."

I looked at Mitzi and she was looking back at me, and a little smile was growing at the corners of her mouth.

Our parents and Velma and Theodore went into the kitchen. Mrs. Bloom was still wiping her eyes and everyone was talking at once.

"Do you want to come to my room?" I asked Mitzi.

She nodded and my chest filled with happiness. My best friend. Nothing could really change that, could it? I shut the door, hoping that Theodore wouldn't come in, too. "I'm sorry," Mitzi said.

"Me too," I answered, surprised that it was so easy.

"Then are you g-l-a-d again?"

"Y-e-s," I spelled.

"Oh, I'm so r-e-l-e-i-v-e-d," Mitzi said.

I almost recited the spelling rule about *i* before *e* except after *c,* but I thought she might get angry again, so I didn't.

Later, when everyone had gone home and Theodore and I were in our beds, I whispered to him, "Theodore? Are you sleeping?"

He didn't answer, but I could hear his breathing and it sounded as if he was still awake.

"Listen," I said. "You're *not* a baby. You're a good kid."

He still didn't answer but he moved around in his bed and he sighed, and I think he was listening.

ten

Double Feature

"I have one cheese and one tuna fish," Mitzi said. "What do you have?"

I opened the bag that my mother had packed. There was a strong spicy smell. "Bologna," I said, without even looking.

It was Saturday, and Mitzi and Theodore and I were going to the movies at the Loew's theater. When we got there, the line was halfway down the block. Most of the other kids had their lunches with them too, because the show at the Loew's was very long, and you were always hungry before it was over. Several of our friends were on the line and one tall person with henna-red hair and a coat with a fox collar stood near the front. It was Mrs. Golub, the only grownup waiting to see the Saturday-afternoon show. She waved and blew us a kiss.

"What's playing?" Theodore asked for the millionth time that day.

"I *told* you," I said, but a few minutes later he asked again. I read aloud to him from the movie marquee. *"Ride 'em Cowboy* and *Lucky Saves the Day."* There was always a double feature on Saturday.

Mitzi sighed. "I wish they had *Bride of Frankenstein* and *The Mummy's Hand* again," she said. She was always disappointed when there wasn't a horror movie. But if there'd been one, Theodore wouldn't have gone with us, because horror movies gave him bad dreams. Once I took him to see one about a mad scientist who made zombies out of ordinary people like teachers and doctors and policemen. They all walked in their sleep with their arms out and their eyes wide open. Theodore sat on the floor under his seat for the whole show, but he still woke during the night yelling about monsters who were trying to get him.

Just when Theodore was starting to get restless, the theater doors opened and the line moved slowly ahead.

Finally we were inside and we got good seats in the third row of the children's section. The lights were still on and we waved and called to our friends.

I could see Mrs. Golub sitting on the other side of the theater in the very first row. Then the lights dimmed slowly and music came from the ceiling. I could hear paper bags rattling—some kids couldn't wait to eat their lunch. The matron for the children's section, a fat lady in a white uniform, flashed her flashlight and told kids to sit down and be quiet. Then the heavy curtain in front of the screen rose as if by magic, in lovely ripples, and we sat back in the dark against the red velvet seats.

The cowboy movie was first. Mitzi and I didn't care very much for Westerns, so we whispered to each other during most of it, but Theodore sat forward with his hands gripping the seat in front of him, as if he were on a fast ride in an amusement park. The movie was about cattle rustlers and a handsome stranger. Everybody thought the handsome stranger had something to do with the rustling, except for the rancher's pretty daughter, who had faith in him. There were a lot of campfires and people shouting and thundering hooves. Somebody kept saying, "After him, men!" The boys in the audience cheered when the ranchers formed a posse and chased the rustlers. But when the handsome stranger put his arm around the rancher's daughter while they were sitting on a fence in the moonlight, some of the boys became restless. And when the stranger began to sing to her, they stood on their seats and hissed and yelled, "Don't kiss her! You'll be sorreee!" and other stuff like that. The matron ran up and down the aisles flashing her light and making them sit down again. Finally the first movie was over and everyone cheered and whistled and clapped.

By then Mitzi and I were hungry and we opened our lunch bags. I gave Theodore a sandwich too. "What's next?" he asked.

"You know," I said. "The cartoon."

The cartoon was about a big mean cat chasing a little mouse. In the end the mouse got away and the cat had lost half his fur and had a lump on his head bigger than Theodore's. Everyone yelled hooray again and then we watched the newsreel. First there was the war news and Mitzi held my hand when they showed some soldiers digging foxholes in Germany. We always looked carefully to see if Buddy was one of the soldiers in the newsreel, but we never saw him. There was a lot of gunfire and there were great flashes of light and I held Mitzi's hand until they showed some movie stars selling bonds to help the war effort.

"What's next?" Theodore asked again.

"The serial," Mitzi told him. "Do you remember last week when the girl was stuck in that giant machine and the bad guy was going to start the motor and she would get all mashed up like a potato? Well, now we're going to see what happens."

That was all Theodore had to hear. He went right down under his seat. "Get up," I whispered to him. "Nothing will happen to the girl. Flash Gordon will save her." But Theodore wouldn't come up until the serial was over. At the end the girl was left dangling over a pit filled with hungry alligators. TO BE CONTINUED appeared across the screen.

Finally the other movie began, the one about the boy and his dog. The boy lived in the country and the dog was always saving his life and helping other little kids and saving old ladies who were stuck in burning buildings. But there was a mean old farmer who wanted to get rid of the dog. When Theodore realized that something bad might happen to that wonderful dog, he began to cry.

"What's the matter?" I said.

But he just sniffled and wiped his nose on his sleeve.

"Nothing is going to happen to the dog, silly," I said. "You'll see."

Mitzi tried to give Theodore one of the oatmeal cookies from her lunch bag, but he wouldn't take his eyes off the movie screen for a second. Sure enough, in the next scene the poor dog ate some poisoned meat that the mean farmer left out for him. Then the dog fell down under a tree and just lay there. "He'll get up soon," I promised Theodore, but I wasn't so sure myself. He certainly *looked* dead. If he wasn't, that dog was some terrific actor.

Then the little boy came whistling through the woods looking for his good old dog. He kept calling the dog's name and whistling for him and there was some scary music in the background. "Uh-*oh!*" Mitzi said, as the boy came closer and closer to the tree where the dog was lying so still. "Don't look," she advised Theodore, who was trembling like a bowl of Jell-O. He put his hand up to his face and covered his eyes. But I guess he just couldn't stand the suspense. His fingers opened like a fan and he peeked through the openings just in time to see the boy discover his dog under the tree.

"Lucky! Lucky!" the boy cried, and Theodore sobbed. Actually he was afraid of dogs in real life. He was always sure they were going to jump up and bite him. But the dog in that movie was more like a person.

I tried to comfort him. "He's not dead," I said. "He only fainted. You'll see. He'll get up any minute."

But the dog just lay there while the boy called his name over and over again.

"It's only a movie," I told Theodore. "It's not *real.*" But I didn't feel so well myself. There was a hard lump in my throat. Could Lucky really be dead?

All over the theater, voices called out, "Lucky, Lucky, get up!"

Then the camera showed a close-up of Lucky and you could see the tiniest twitching of his tail. "Yay! Yay!" everyone shouted. It was so noisy we couldn't hear what the boy was saying as he hugged Lucky.

Theodore stood up to get a better look. Lucky was alive!

"Do you see?" I said, as if I had known it all along. "Didn't I tell you he wasn't dead?"

For the first time that day, Theodore smiled. Then we all went outside again, squinting in the bright blaze of sunlight, still thinking about the movie, a little surprised to find we were still in Brooklyn and in our real lives.

eleven

Cure No. 2: The Power of the Mind

"Yoo-hoo, Shirley! Little boy, yoo-hoo! Wait for me!" It was Mrs. Golub coming up the street behind us.

"Who's that?" Mitzi asked.

"Mrs. Golub, the movie lady," I said. "She lives in our building."

"You mean she's in the *movies?*" Mitzi asked.

"Oh, no," I said. "Nothing like that. She's just the biggest movie-star fan in America, that's all."

I didn't say anything else because Mrs. Golub, running

in little choppy steps like a chicken, had caught up with us. She was all out of breath. "Huh-huh," she panted. "Wasn't that movie—huh-huh—just grand?"

We all nodded and I introduced Mitzi to Mrs. Golub, who said she would probably photograph very well, with her blond hair and all. Then she asked if we'd like to come upstairs with her and see her collection of Hollywood souvenirs and pictures.

Mitzi and I looked at each other. "Well, maybe we could come up for a little while," I said. "I don't want my mother to be worried about us."

When we got to our building, the three of us followed Mrs. Golub into apartment 3H. We had never seen another apartment like it. It looked something like the lobby of the Loew's theater. There were photographs everywhere, even on the kitchen walls. Some of them were lit by colored light bulbs and they were all signed. Best wishes, Robert Taylor. Good luck! Greer Garson. Sincerely, Tyrone Power.

Theodore kept walking around with his mouth wide open. He looked at the great big Shirley Temple doll sitting on the living-room sofa, and at the painted pillow that had a picture of palm trees on it. *Souvenir of Hollywood, California, Movie Capital of the World.*

Then, in the hallway, he found a photograph of Lucky, the dog star of the movie we had seen that afternoon.

Lucky was sitting with one paw lifted, as if he was offering to shake hands. Theodore just stood there staring up at the picture.

"Sit down," Mrs. Golub invited. "Make yourselves comfortable. I'll show you girls some of my albums and scrapbooks." Then she opened a closet that was filled with books and papers. There must have been hundreds of them, but Mrs. Golub seemed to know where everything was. She just reached in and pulled out a handful.

Then the three of us sat down on the sofa next to Shirley Temple, who was wearing a beautiful pale-blue dress with a million pleats. First we looked through an album called *Favorite Scenes*. It was filled with still photos from movies Mrs. Golub had seen and liked best. She described them to us as we turned the pages. "That's Clark," she said. "That's Vivien standing next to him. That's Jimmy coming out of prison. There's Pat. He always tries to help Jimmy go straight. There's Lana. Isn't she gorgeous?"

"Very nice," I said, trying to be polite. At first the pictures were interesting, but after a while I began to be tired of them. I looked at Mitzi and I could see she was trying to swallow a yawn. "We'll have to be going home soon, Mrs. Golub," I said. "My mother . . ."

"Oh, girls, you have to see this one before you go. This is my most priceless collection." She pushed a very large scrapbook across our laps. *Secrets of the Stars* was written in big red letters on the cover. Mrs. Golub turned to the first page. It said:

> *Robert's Secret Formula for Success*
> 1. Don't give up. Try, try again.
> 2. Remember that God helps those who help themselves.
> 3. A penny saved is a penny earned.

They didn't sound like real secrets to me. Our parents and our teachers were always saying things like that.

Mrs. Golub turned the page. The Secret of Joan's Peaches and Cream Complexion. "Grade A," Mrs. Golub said.

"What?" Mitzi asked.

"Milk baths," Mrs. Golub whispered, as if someone else was listening. "She takes a milk bath every single night."

"Ukk!" Mitzi said, making a terrible face.

But Mrs. Golub just went on to the next page. Dick's Victory Over Stage Fright. "That's how Dick uses the Power of the Mind to overcome his fears."

"What's the Power of the Mind?" I asked.

"Oh, you know, honey," Mrs. Golub said. "It's like hypnosis, saying over and over again, I won't be afraid, I won't be afraid, until you believe it."

"Does it really work?" Mitzi asked.

"Of course," Mrs. Golub said. "Does Dick ever look frightened to you?" We had to admit that he never did.

I turned around and saw that Theodore was still standing in the hallway looking up at Lucky's picture.

Mrs. Golub looked at him too. "Do you like that picture, sweetie?"

Theodore nodded.

"Well, I have doubles on that one, so I'll give you a copy." She went to another closet and pulled out a photo of Lucky exactly like the one on the wall. "Here," she said, handing it to Theodore.

"Th-thank you," he said, staring at the picture as if he couldn't believe it was his.

I nudged Mitzi and both of us stood up at once. "Goodbye," I said to Mrs. Golub. "It was really very interesting. Thank you for inviting us."

"Me too," Mitzi said.

"Me too," Theodore echoed, clutching his picture.

Back in our apartment we discovered a note from my father.

Dear Shirley and Ted,

Mother and Velma and I are going shopping. See you later.

Love,
Daddy

Mitzi and I went into the kitchen to get some milk and cupcakes, while Theodore took his precious picture into the bedroom. Mitzi sat at the kitchen table wearing a milk mustache and a thoughtful expression. "I have an idea," she said at last.

"What?"

"Oh, something we can do to help Theodore."

"Well, it better not be like the last idea you had," I said. "I don't want to get into trouble again."

"Oh no," Mitzi said. "This is entirely different, and I know it will work. In fact, it was Mrs. Golub who gave me the idea."

"Mrs. Golub?"

"Well, she didn't *know* she gave me the idea. Just something she told us. About the Secrets of the Stars?"

"Do you mean the milk bath?" I was getting worried. Besides, there were only two quarts of milk in the refrigerator.

"No, silly," Mitzi said. "I mean the Power of the Mind. Don't you remember?"

I was still worried. "What do you mean?"

"I mean we'll hypnotize Theodore into believing that he's brave, that's all."

"We don't know anything about hypnotizing people," I said.

"Oh, that's nothing," Mitzi assured me. "It can't be

73

very hard. A long time ago my father and I saw a hypnotist on the stage at the Roxy. Marvello the Great. I remember pretty much what he did and it didn't look that hard. We just have to get Theodore into a trance."

I bit my lip. "I don't know, maybe . . ."

"Maybe it will just be the best thing we've ever done," Mitzi said. "You heard Mrs. Golub. The Power of the Mind. Shirley, we could become famous. I can just see the headlines in the newspapers. Brooklyn Girls Save Little Brother from Being a Sissy."

"Well . . ." I said.

Before I could say anything else, Mitzi went into the hallway and called Theodore. "Theodore?" she said in a very sweet voice. "Wouldn't you like a nice chocolate cupcake? Creamy and delicious? A nice cold glass of yummy milk?"

Theodore came out of the bedroom and followed her to the kitchen. Mitzi was just like the Pied Piper of Hamelin. She poured a big foaming glass of milk for him and put the whole box of cupcakes right in front of him. "Go ahead," she said generously. "Pick one with a lot of icing on it. Then when you're finished, we'll play this little game."

"Wh-what kind of game?" Theodore asked.

"Oh, something nice," Mitzi said. "You'll like it. Hurry up now and get finished."

I wondered when my parents and Velma would be home. Could Mitzi really hypnotize Theodore?

She was certainly going to try. Theodore still had cupcake crumbs all over his mouth when she led him into the living room and made him lie down on the sofa.

"I-I don't want to p-play that g-ghost game again," he said.

"Oh no," Mitzi said in that same sweet voice. "You'll really love this game. All you have to do is just listen to me and do what I tell you. Okay?"

"O-okay," he said.

Mitzi pulled a chair close to the sofa and sat down. I cleared my throat and she turned around and said, "Shhhh. Quiet. It must be absolutely quiet or the Power of the Mind won't work." She turned back to Theodore again. "Now look at me," she told him. "Look into my eyes." She opened her own blue eyes wide and leaned her face close to his.

Theodore began to giggle.

"Quiet!" she commanded. "This is very serious."

"I-I thought it was a g-game," Theodore said.

"Well, it is. Only it's a serious game. You have to concentrate or it won't work."

She leaned close again and stared into his eyes. Theodore put his hand over his mouth to hold back another fit of the giggles.

"Theodore, look into my eyes," Mitzi said. "Listen to the sound of my voice. You are going into a trance."

Theodore sat up. "What's a t-trance?" he said.

"It's . . . it's . . . never mind what it is. Just lie down again. You are going to listen to nothing but my voice. You are going to obey only my voice."

"Okay," Theodore said.

"Shhh. You're not supposed to answer me. Just look deeply into my eyes."

Theodore stared back at Mitzi. He blinked and he yawned.

"You are going to be in my power," Mitzi said. "You will do anything I tell you."

Theodore yawned again, forgetting to cover his mouth.

"Soon, soon, you will be in a trance. Now shut your eyes," Mitzi said. "Shut your eyes and listen only to the sound of my voice."

Theodore closed his eyes.

"Ah, good," Mitzi said, turning around for a second to smile at me. "Now, raise your right hand," she said. "Raise it slowly."

"He doesn't know which is his right," I whispered.

Mitzi said "Shhh" again, putting her finger to her lips.

Sure enough, Theodore raised his left hand. He turned onto his side and yawned again.

"Now you are under the Power of My Mind," Mitzi said, speaking very slowly. "You are in a deep, deep trance. You will do everything I tell you to do. Listen to the sound of my voice, Theodore. You are going to be a brave boy from now on. You are going to be stronger than Superman, faster than Flash Gordon, braver than Lucky, the dog actor. Theodore, I want you to sit up now."

Theodore just lay there with his eyes shut.

"Theodore," Mitzi said, a little louder this time. "I want you to sit up!"

"He's asleep," I said.

"He is not!" Mitzi insisted. "He's in a trance."

"Well, he *looks* just like he does when he's asleep." And he did. Theodore had his knees drawn up and one hand resting under his chin, and he was breathing evenly.

"I want you to sit up right now!" Mitzi was really yelling this time.

Theodore went on sleeping.

"He's hard to wake up in the morning, too," I said.

"It's not *my* fault," Mitzi said. "I did the very same things as Marvello the Great. I guess it just doesn't work on first-grade babies."

She sounded as if she was getting angry. "You can hypnotize *me* if you want to," I offered.

"I would," Mitzi said, "but I have to go home now."

She marched past Theodore and put on her coat.

Later, when my mother and father and Velma came home from shopping, Theodore was just getting up from his nap. "Where's Mitzi?" he wanted to know. "That was a g-good game."

twelve

The First Round

It was the big day. All the way to school, hard words went in and out of my head. "Shirley," Theodore kept saying, pulling on the sleeve of my coat, but I wouldn't answer him. I was too busy practicing for the first round of the spelling bee. It was going to take place that very afternoon in Dr. Vanderbilt's office. In the office with the door marked D. M. VANDERBILT, PRINCIPAL, where you usually had to go only if you were in some terrible trouble.

Before I left the house, Mother kissed me on both cheeks for luck, just like a French general. Daddy kissed the top of my head. "We're proud of you, Shirley-girl," he said. Even Velma came out of the bathroom, where she had been brushing her teeth. She still had her toothbrush in her hand. "Good luck, Shirley," she said. "Make the Bravermans famous in Brooklyn." Then she kissed me too, a wet kiss that smelled nicely of mint toothpaste.

But I was very nervous, more nervous than I ever was before a test, or when I had to go to the dentist to have a cavity filled. I felt the corn flakes and sliced banana I'd had for breakfast dancing around in my belly.

I was glad to see Mitzi waiting for me as soon as I reached the schoolyard. "I brought my good-luck charm for you to borrow," she said. She pressed something cold and hard into my hand. I looked down and saw Mitzi's favorite bracelet, a gold circle with a tiny Scotty dog charm hanging from it. Buddy had bought it for her just before he joined the Army. He called it a going-away present, even though he was the one who was going away.

"Oh, Mitzi," I said. "I can't . . ."

"You *have* to. It will bring you good luck. I want you to wear it."

So I slipped the gold bracelet onto my wrist. It looked beautiful there.

One other kid in our class, a boy named Sheldon

Bloch, was going to enter the spelling competition. He looked just as nervous as I felt. All the other boys were standing around him. I knew they were going to root for Sheldon to win that afternoon, just the way the girls were going to root for me. There were going to be ten kids in this first spelling bee, some from each sixth-grade class. Nobody else but the five teachers and the principal would be present, but all the friends of the kids who were in it were going to wait in the schoolyard for the results.

"I'm going to keep my fingers crossed," Mitzi said, "and my arms," she added, twisting them around one another, "and my feet, and my . . ."

I looked at her and saw that she had crossed her eyes as well. "Stop it," I said. "I'm too nervous to laugh."

"Don't be nervous, Shirley," Mitzi said. "I know you're going to win. I just *know* it."

But I imagined that Sheldon Bloch's friends were telling him the very same thing, that *his* mother and father had kissed him for luck that morning. I knew that all the kids were hoping to win and there would only be one winner.

How could I concentrate on anything but the spelling bee? Miss Cohen put arithmetic problems on the blackboard. If it takes six men two days to build a bridge, how many days would it take . . . I couldn't think about the numbers at all. I just kept thinking about those six men high above the sparkling water of the river, putting the pieces of the bridge together.

Miss Cohen was walking around the room, looking at our papers while we worked.

Six men. Two days. Bang! Bang! Over here, Joe! Lower that girder, Mac!

When Miss Cohen leaned over my shoulder, my paper was still as white as snow. I thought she would be angry and say something about daydreaming. But instead I felt her hand resting lightly on my shoulder. "Don't worry, Shirley," she said. "I know you're going to do well today. Just do the best you can. We're all proud of you, whether you win or not."

"I'm wearing Mitzi's good-luck charm," I said, holding my arm up to show her.

"That was nice of her," Miss Cohen said, "but you have to depend on your good sense and not be superstitious. Sometimes you make your own good luck."

I nodded, feeling much better. The rest of the day wasn't so bad. I felt better and better until the moment I faced Dr. Vanderbilt's closed door. All at once my hands were sweaty and cold, and I could feel the thump of my heart.

Then the door opened and I went inside with the others. One by one we approached Dr. Vanderbilt's desk.

He shook hands with each of us and said, Good luck! in a deep and special voice, the way I imagined King Ferdinand said it to Christopher Columbus before he set out to find a new way to India. When it was my turn, I wiped my hand on my shirt first, but he must have felt how cold it was, because he squeezed it very hard and smiled at me.

The five teachers were going to be judges. They sat at a long table on the other side of the office. The ten of us who were going to be in the spelling bee stood facing Dr. Vanderbilt's desk. A sealed envelope rested on top of it.

"Boys and girls," he said. "In a few moments we are going to begin. I want you all to know that P.S. 247 is very proud of you. You are all fine students, and the future of our great country depends on you. *Ahem. Ahem.*"

When he cleared his throat, I knew the spelling bee was about to begin. Sure enough, Dr. Vanderbilt picked up the envelope and opened it with a silver letter opener. Then he sat back in his chair, reading the list of words to himself. "Your teachers have prepared this list from a selection of the more advanced words for the sixth-grade student. Again, good luck to all of you. If a student misses a word, the next student must try to spell the same word. As soon as it is spelled correctly, the one who missed will be eliminated from the bee. If a student is eliminated, he or she will sit here until a winner is officially declared."

He indicated with his hand a row of chairs lined up against the wall behind us.

"The first word is 'progress.' The student is making good *progress* with his work. 'Progress.'"

The first boy on the line stepped forward and spelled it correctly. Dr. Vanderbilt turned to a girl from the room across from ours. "'Business,'" he said to her. "My father's *business* has earned a good profit. 'Business.'"

At the end of the first round, nobody was eliminated. My word was easy. "Electric." I took a very deep breath after I spelled it, and felt better.

In the second round, one of the boys was caught on the word "attendant"; he put an *e* near the end instead of an *a*. I could see that the words were getting a little harder. Yet I came through the second round and the third and the fourth. Another boy and two girls had been eliminated by then, and the words were getting even harder.

After seven rounds there were only three of us left. Sheldon Bloch from my class, Antoinette Scarpi, a tall dark-haired girl, and myself.

I touched the little Scotty dog on Mitzi's bracelet. Then I remembered what Miss Cohen had said about making your own good luck. I listened as Antoinette tried to spell "vacuum."

"'Vacuum,'" she said. "V-a-c-c-u-m."

"I'm sorry, Antoinette," Dr. Vanderbilt said. "That is not correct."

I looked at Antoinette and saw her blush and lower her eyes. Even though we were in competition with one another, I felt sorry for her.

Now the next person in the line had to spell "vacuum." That was Sheldon. If he couldn't spell it right, it would be my turn. If I could do it correctly, I would be the winner! And I knew how to spell "vacuum." It was one of my favorites in *Words That Stump the Experts*.

" 'Vacuum,' " Sheldon said, his voice cracking a little in the middle of the word. "V-a-c-u-u-m."

"Very good!" Dr. Vanderbilt said, and he nodded at Antoinette, who took a seat against the wall.

Now there were just two of us. Sheldon and me. Dr. Vanderbilt turned to me. " 'Rhythm,' " he said. "The orchestra has very good *rhythm*. 'Rhythm.' "

Oh dear. Why was I so nervous again? I had to concentrate. It was a word I had studied. I took a deep breath and let it out slowly, something I always advised Theodore to do to help him relax. " 'Rhythm,' " I said. "R-h-y-t-h-m."

"Very good!" Dr. Vanderbilt said and I said, "Whew!" right out loud, which made him smile again.

Then Sheldon missed a word I had never studied. "Chauffeur." I could hear Dr. Vanderbilt say, "I'm sorry, Sheldon. That isn't the correct spelling. Please wait and we will see if Shirley can spell it."

" 'Chauffeur,' " I said aloud. The room was very quiet. The five teachers looked at me with serious faces, like five judges in a courtroom. How had Sheldon spelled it anyway? I couldn't even remember. It was a nice word, full of soft sounds. "C," I began, "h-a-u." Was it one *f* or two? I imagined a tall handsome chauffeur tipping his hat as I entered a limousine. Good evening, madam.

"F," I said, and paused. "F-e-u-r." I shut my eyes and held my breath. Nobody said anything for what seemed like a very long time.

"Congratulations, Shirley!" When I opened my eyes Dr. Vanderbilt was standing behind his desk holding his hand out to me. I took it. I was the winner! Me! I was the best speller in P.S. 247!

Then Dr. Vanderbilt shook Sheldon's hand too, and Sheldon said, "CongratulationsShirley," as if it were just one long word, and I guessed that his mother had told him to say that to whoever won, if it wasn't him.

"Thank you, thank you!" I said. The other kids gathered around me and Miss Cohen came over and gave me a hug. "Room 155 did very well today," she said, including Sheldon in her smile.

Then I was outdoors again and the air had never seemed so sweet. I raced across the schoolyard, toward the little groups of kids waiting to hear the results of the spelling bee. As I ran I felt as if I were flying, as if my legs weren't moving at all. I could see Mitzi running toward me, ahead of the other girls, her arms stretched out. "You won, oh Shirley, you won!" Her voice came across the yard to me, and even after the words were lost in the wind, I still heard them over and over again inside my head.

thirteen

Hidden Treasure

"What do you want to do?" Mitzi asked.

"I don't know. What do you want to do?"

Mitzi paused for a moment with one finger pressed against her face. "I don't know. What do you want to do?"

Velma took the book she was reading and slammed it face-down on the arm of her chair. "If you girls say that one more time, I'm going to scream!"

"Well, we really don't have anything to do," I said. I guess I whined a little when I said it. It was a rainy

Sunday afternoon and Mother and Daddy had gone to visit Grandpa Small without either of us. He was sicker than he had ever been before and Mother said he was much too weak for any extra company.

Theodore and Arthur, another little boy who lived in our building, were pushing toy cars and trucks under the skirts of the living-room sofa and chairs. They were making motor noises with their mouths and calling each other Jim and Bill for their game. "Jim, deliver this here cement to 162 Brooklyn Avenue." "Okay, Bill."

"Nothing to do?" Velma said in her bossiest voice. "Why, there's *plenty* you can do."

"Name one thing," I said.

Velma looked thoughtful. "Why, you could do some extra schoolwork."

Mitzi made her fainting face, rolling her eyes up so only the white parts showed, and letting her tongue hang out.

"Well," Velma said, pretending she couldn't even see Mitzi. "You could knit some afghan squares for the Red Cross."

"Me?" I said. "The way I knit? It would have so many holes, the poor person who used it would end up with double pneumonia."

"You girls will just have to think up something yourselves," Velma said, picking up her book again. "I want to see what happens to poor Jane Eyre."

"J-Jim," Theodore said to his friend Arthur. "Get this truckload of coal over to the lady's house."

"Right, Bill," Arthur said. "Lady, where is your coal chute?"

Mitzi and I went into the kitchen. The rain slanted against the window and dark clouds rolled across the sky. I opened the refrigerator and looked inside. "Do you want an apple?"

"No, thank you," Mitzi said. "I'm not hungry. I'm just bored, bored, bored."

I shut the refrigerator. I wasn't really hungry either.

"Sunday is my worst day," Mitzi said. "Especially if it rains and I can't go outside."

"Yes. In books, people always live in those big old houses with attics and basements, and when it rains they go looking for hidden treasure."

"That's right," Mitzi said. "There's always some old trunk with valuable papers inside that prove somebody in jail is innocent or something."

"Or that the mean old man on the other side of town is really their grandfather. And when he finds out, he's not mean any more."

"Well, I'm not going to look for any hidden treasure in *your* basement. That place is really haunted."

"Oh, it's not so bad," I said. "The ghosts are all friendly. Ha-ha."

"Ha-ha," Mitzi echoed in a tiny voice.

"But," I said, "we could look in a closet for something."

Mitzi looked interested. "For what?"

"I don't know," I said, wishing I could think of something. Mitzi always had the best ideas.

"Maybe we'll find out that Dr. Vanderbilt is really your long-lost uncle," she suggested.

We both giggled. But then Mitzi said, "Are you sure your mother won't get mad if we snoop around in the closets?"

"Of course not," I said. "At least, she *probably* won't, especially if we do a little spring cleaning at the same time."

"A little *what?*"

"Cleaning. You know, straighten things out and make them neat."

"I don't know . . ." Mitzi said. She hated housework and her mother was always complaining that Mitzi's room looked like it had been hit by a tornado.

"Who knows?" I said. "Maybe we'll find a valuable letter from George Washington or Abe Lincoln."

"Or a five-thousand-dollar bill stuck in an old envelope."

"Or a gigantic diamond ring that my mother forgot she had."

We were both laughing so hard that we almost forgot it was a rainy Sunday afternoon with nothing to do.

The hall closet seemed like the right place to begin our investigation. That was where Mother always put the things we couldn't find any other place for. When the hall closet was completely filled, my mother and father would make a trip to the basement, where each family had a storage bin to keep the junk they couldn't bear to throw away.

In the closet, Mitzi and I found boxes filled with old report cards and autograph albums and birthday cards. Mother kept her wedding dress in there as well. It was in a blue zippered garment bag filled with moth balls. Mitzi and I unzipped it halfway and put our hands in to touch the creamy satin of the long skirt. At the bottom of the bag, wrapped in tissue paper, were Mother's wedding veil and headpiece.

When Velma and I were very little, even before Theodore was born, Mother let us each have a chance to dress up and play bride, while Daddy sang "Here Comes the Bride" at the top of his lungs. First Velma walked down the "aisle," which was really only the long hallway at the entrance to our apartment, and I walked behind her, holding up the train. I thought it was the funniest word I had ever heard for a part of a dress and I remember that Mother and Daddy laughed when I said, "Chooo chooo," as I walked behind Velma. Mother had made a bouquet of tissue-paper flowers and candy-box ribbons. Of course there was no one there for us to pretend to marry when we got to the end of the "aisle" and landed in the kitchen.

"Oh, what beautiful brides you'll be," Mother said, clasping her hands together under her chin.

Daddy smiled and said, "If you take my advice, young ladies, you'll elope!" He had to explain how that meant running away to get married, and Mother became very upset. "It's only a joke, Etta," he said, putting his arm around her waist and pulling her close to him. "They *will* be beautiful brides."

When it was my turn to get dressed, the wedding veil kept slipping over one ear, but I thought I looked splendid anyway. Ta-da te-dum! Here comes the bride . . .

"Let's look for the diamonds and the money," Mitzi said now, zipping the garment bag and pushing it back in place. She knew I wouldn't take the wedding dress out unless Mother was home.

But we did find other clothes we could try on: old hats and shoes and things that Mother had put aside for the War Relief Rummage Sale the PTA was going to hold at the school that week.

"Oh, you look simply gorgeous, dahling," Mitzi said when I pulled a gray beret down over one eye.

She tried to walk around on Mother's old platform

ankle-strap shoes, but her ankles wobbled and her feet kept turning over on their sides.

Then Velma came in with her book still in her hand. I thought she was going to start yelling at us for making a mess, but instead she took a big-brimmed straw hat with one drooping pink rose on its crown and put it on. She really looked pretty. Was it possible that my sister Velma was *pretty?* "You look nice," I said.

"Oh, do you really think so? Here, let me fix that. You have to get just the right angle with a beret. There, that's perfect. You look sweet, Shirley."

We were nicer to one another than we had been in a long, long time.

Velma helped Mitzi to button the back of a tea-rose crepe evening gown, and then she suggested a little dusty-pink lipstick and some matching nail polish, which she said she just happened to have in her room. I have to admit that I did look in the drawers of Velma's dresser once in a while, but I had never found lipstick or nail polish there. All I ever saw was her underwear and her pajamas and her socks, all folded neatly in little piles. Of course, whenever Velma caught me, she always started yelling about her precious things. The nail polish and lipstick were under one of the neat piles of underpants in Velma's dresser drawer. Mitzi still bit her fingernails pretty close, so Velma could just put a tiny dab of polish on each one. But they looked nice, anyway. Then Velma put some lipstick and nail polish on me too and she said that I had very artistic hands.

I felt happy and embarrassed at the same time. "By the way," I said, just to change the subject, "what happened to Jane?"

"Who?"

"Jane, in your book."

"Oh. Jane *Eyre*. She lived happily ever after," Velma said.

From the other room we could hear "Jim" and "Bill" calling to one another, and outside the rain beat the same light rhythm against the windows. Only now it seemed pleasant and cozy in the apartment instead of boring and dreary. Mitzi didn't even mind that there had been no real hidden treasure, no diamonds or money or secret papers. And she helped with the cleaning part of the agreement, standing on a stepstool while we handed boxes up to her.

"That looks good. Mother will be surprised," Velma said.

But I was the one who was really surprised. For a little while Velma and I had been friends.

fourteen
Mirror, Mirror on the Wall

Feb 15, 1945

Dear Peewee,

It was so much fun getting a letter from you. How could you think I would forget who you are? Of course I know that you and Mitz are growing up and I have been away for such a long time. When I come home you girls will have to wear red roses in your hair, so I'll be sure to recognize you!

Mitzi wrote and said that you are the champion speller in your school and that you will probably end up being the champion of all New York City. I'm sure she's right. Spelling was never my best subject and I hope you don't find too many mistakes in this letter.

Well, Peewee, take good care of yourself and if you have time, I would enjoy hearing from you again. Good luck in everything you do.

Love from
Buddy

Love from Buddy. Love, love, love. Everybody watched me when I took the thin V-mail letter from the kitchen table. But I went into the bathroom to read it, feeling excited and nervous. Love from Buddy. He said that Mitzi and I should wear red roses in our hair so he would be sure to recognize us. That sounded so romantic! I looked into the mirror above the sink. Would I really look that different when Buddy came home? The funny thing was you never saw the changes in yourself, even though you were changing and growing every single minute of the day. Buddy said that I would probably be the champion speller in all of New York City. That made me feel very proud. Somebody far, far away across the ocean had faith in me.

"Mirror, mirror on the wall,
  Who is the greatest speller of them all?"

Of course I didn't say who is the *fairest* of them all, the way Snow White's stepmother did. I knew I wasn't bad-looking and I thought that if my hair was blond instead of brown, if I had dimples and if my nose was a little different, I might even look a tiny bit like Shirley Temple. Yet I had to admit that I wasn't the fairest in the land.

But spelling! Buddy had written that letter three weeks ago and he didn't even know what had happened since then. A few days before, I had won the district-wide spelling competition against kids from eight other schools. It was very close, though. A boy named Alvin Michael Jones from P.S. 205 went right down the line with me. When everyone else was eliminated (with two of the girls crying like babies), Alvin and I just spelled one hard word after another. This time the bee was held in the auditorium of a neighborhood school, and the superintendent of the district was the one who read the words to us. The principals of all the schools were the judges.

Before the bee, Dr. Vanderbilt gave me another speech about being the pride of the school and the future of America, etc., etc. The auditorium was filled with teachers and parents and friends of all the contestants. Theodore had to sit on my father's lap.

When only Alvin and I were left, neither of us made a mistake for what seemed like forever. Once in a while you could hear a tiny gasp from the audience or a nervous cough, but they had been told not to clap or cheer until the winner was declared. It looked as if we would be there all day, but then Alvin had trouble with the word "bookkeeper," the only word I know of in the English language with three sets of double letters, one right after the other. He was so mad that he didn't even congratulate me when I spelled it correctly. He just went stomping off the stage muttering about girls who think they're so smart.

Of course the audience cheered and applauded all at once, and it sounded strange to me, like a great roar, like the ocean sound you hear in a seashell. A hundred people came up to shake hands with me and flashbulbs kept going off.

The next day my picture was in the newspaper. Underneath, it said:

BENSONHURST GIRL IS
WINNER IN DISTRICT-WIDE SPELLING BEE

Shirley Braverman, a sixth-grade student at P.S. 247, took first place in a spelling bee held yesterday at P.S.

143 in Brooklyn. The runner-up, Alvin Michael Jones of P.S. 205, was defeated on the tricky word "bookkeeper." Miss Braverman, an attractive young lady with curly brown hair and sparkling brown eyes, told a reporter for this newspaper that her secret formula for success was to study hard. She will go on to compete for the mayor's medal in a competition to determine the best speller in all of New York City.

I didn't even remember talking to a reporter! And that secret formula didn't sound any more mysterious than the ones in Mrs. Golub's *Secrets of the Stars* album.

My father bought ten copies of the newspaper with my picture in it and he taped the page to the front of the refrigerator. Every time I went to get a glass of milk or an apple, my own face smiled back at me. BENSONHURST GIRL IS WINNER . . .

I talked about it at dinner and after dinner, and even after Theodore and I were in bed. I talked about how great it felt standing up on that stage . . . Theodore made loud snoring noises as if he were asleep, but I knew that he was only fooling, so I just went on talking.

The next morning at breakfast, I went right to the refrigerator to get the oranges and to sneak another look at the newspaper article.

Velma was very grouchy at the breakfast table. Right

after the bee she had been as nice as she could be, congratulating me and saying how wonderful it was that I had won. But at breakfast she started picking on me for leaving the cap off the toothpaste and not helping with the supper dishes the night before. Was Velma jealous of me?

I was standing in front of the mirror, holding Buddy's letter and thinking about it all. "Mirror, mirror on the wall . . ."

And there was Velma again, standing in the doorway watching me. Velma the spy, always sneaking up when you least expected her. "Are you talking to yourself?" she asked.

"What?" I said, pretending that I was doing something to my hair. I didn't have a comb or brush, so I sort of combed it with my fingers.

"Are you talking to yourself?" Velma said again.

"Of course not. Can't you see, I'm just combing my hair."

"Oh? Without a comb? Besides, I heard somebody talking in here."

What an old snoop! "Well, it wasn't me," I said.

"Anyway," Velma said. "Somebody is getting very conceited around this house."

"I am *not!*"

"I never said *who* was getting conceited," Velma said,

in her meanest voice. "You must have a guilty conscience."

I opened my mouth, but before I could say anything, she said, "Just remember, Shirley Braverman, that pride goeth before a fall." And she marched away with her nose up in the air.

Well! What was that supposed to mean anyway? Pride goeth before a fall. People were always saying things like that to me. All that glitters is not gold. A stitch in time saves nine. Don't count your chickens before they hatch. Proverbs. She was just jealous because *her* picture wasn't in the newspaper, because *she* wasn't famous in Bensonhurst. Somehow, I knew that wasn't really true. After all, she *had* been nice about my winning in the first place. She only seemed mean when I wouldn't stop talking about it, when I couldn't help bragging and looking at my own picture all day. I sighed, a long sad sigh like the sound of air going out of a balloon.

When I looked in the mirror again, trying to find the future best speller in the whole wide world, that attractive young lady with curly brown hair and sparkling brown eyes, I only saw myself, Shirley Braverman of Brooklyn, New York, as if a magic spell had been broken.

fifteen
Big Brother Harry

After I received that letter from Buddy, nobody heard from him at all. Weeks and weeks went by without any V-mail. Sometimes Mrs. Bloom went downstairs to wait for the mailman an hour before he was due to arrive. Then he brought only bills and magazines and advertisements. There was no mail from Buddy and the whole Bloom family was worried. From the news we heard on the radio and read in the papers, it looked as if the war in Europe might end pretty soon. But still the soldiers were fighting very hard and some of them were being killed or wounded.

Mitzi became quieter and quieter and I knew she was thinking about her brother and what might have happened to him. She hardly ever made jokes any more, or funny faces. I tried to cheer her up, but I didn't feel so cheerful myself. I was worried too.

One day, when Theodore and I came home from school, Velma was sitting in the kitchen drinking a glass of milk and painting her toenails at the same time. "Something came for you in the mail," she said.

My heart fluttered. "What?" I asked. If only it was a letter from Buddy!

Velma shrugged. "I don't know. I put it on your bed."

I ran into the bedroom, dropping my school books on the way. But when I got there, there was no thin blue V-mail envelope. Just a great big fat brown one addressed to S. Braverman. At first I was puzzled, and then, as I opened the flap, I remembered that day with Mitzi and the coupon we had sent to King Sandor.

Sure enough, it was the free instruction booklet. I sat on the edge of the bed and opened it. What a disappointment! There were just some black and white drawings of gigantic dumbbells and punching bags and a couple of heavy-looking exercise machines that King Sandor was selling. And the prices! There wasn't a thing in that booklet that Mitzi and I could afford, even if we saved our allowance for a year.

There was something else inside the plain brown envelope, though. It was the free photograph of King Sandor himself. His muscles looked bigger than ever and he was holding up a tremendous dumbbell with one hand, as if it didn't weigh any more than a lollipop. At the bottom of the picture, written in script, was "Yours for a better body, King Sandor."

I couldn't wait until Mitzi came over that afternoon so I could show it to her. Of course she was disappointed about the instruction booklet too. It didn't look as if we were going to help Theodore get big muscles after all. Mitzi kept staring at the picture of King Sandor and tapping her fingers on the dresser top. "I've got an idea!" she said finally.

"What?"

"Never mind," she said. "I'll explain later. Do you know what that boy looks like?"

"What boy?"

"The one who picks on Theodore."

"Oh, him. Sure. He has red hair and lots of freckles. His name is Stanley something."

Mitzi tucked the picture back into the envelope. "Come on," she said.

"But where?"

"To the schoolyard. Let's see if that boy Stanley is there."

I wanted to ask a million questions but Mitzi was through the doorway before I could think. Besides, she had been very mopey lately and this was the first time in a while she showed any interest in anything but Buddy. I hated to spoil it by asking too many questions.

I had to walk pretty fast all the way to the schoolyard, just to keep up with her. Over in one corner some girls from our grade were jumping double-Dutch rope. They waved to us and called, and I think they were going to ask us to play too, but Mitzi just waved back and kept on walking. On the other side of the schoolyard a lot of boys were shooting baskets. "Is he here?" Mitzi asked. "Do you see that Stanley?"

I moved closer, searching carefully in the running crowd of boys, and there he was! He was taller than the others and his red hair stuck straight up in spikes all over his head. "That's him," I told Mitzi. "What are you going to do now?"

Mitzi took my hand and pulled me right over under the basket. The ball bounced through and almost hit me on the head. "Hey, watch out!" one of the boys said. "Get off the court! Hey, somebody get those stupid girls off the court!"

Mitzi marched right up to Stanley, not paying any

attention to the other boys, who were all yelling at us by then. "Are you Stanley?" she demanded.

The redheaded boy puffed out his chest and made a terrible face. No wonder Theodore was afraid of him! "Who wants to know?" he demanded.

"I do," Mitzi said.

"Oh, yeah?"

"Yeah!"

"Well, I'm Stanley."

"Do you pick on a skinny little kid named Theodore who's only in the first grade? Do you tell him you're going to give him an Indian burn if he doesn't give you his baseball cards?"

"Well, what if I do?"

"You're a big bully, that's what! And you better leave that kid alone or else!" Mitzi sounded almost as tough as Stanley, but he didn't seem to be afraid of her. He just hitched up his trousers and smirked.

"Who says so?" he asked.

"*I* do," Mitzi answered.

"Me too," I said, but not half as loud as Mitzi.

"You and who else?" Stanley said, looking meaner than ever.

"Me and Theodore's older brother," Mitzi said.

I was so surprised I almost said "Who?" myself. But Stanley said it for me.

Mitzi stuck her hand inside the brown envelope then and pulled out the big picture of King Sandor. She kept her fingers over the place where he'd written "Yours for a better body" and signed his name. "That's who!" she said, pushing the picture right under Stanley's nose. "That's Theodore's older brother, er . . . Harry, and he just happens to be a policeman and he told me to find out who's been picking on his little brother!"

I looked at Mitzi in amazement. She had never told so many lies at one time in her life.

Stanley seemed pretty surprised too. His mouth fell open and he looked down at his feet. "Awww," he said. "Can't that kid take a joke?"

"A joke!" Mitzi said. "Do you call scaring a little first-grader a *joke?*"

"Awww," Stanley said again. "I was only fooling around. I didn't mean anything."

"Well," Mitzi said. "I certainly hope not. But you'd better leave Theodore alone, or I'll just have to point you out to old Harry." She waved the photograph in his face again.

The other boys were dribbling the basketball, waiting for us to get off the court. Somehow, Stanley didn't look as tall or as mean any more. He kept kicking at the cement with the toe of his sneaker while Mitzi and I walked across the court and out of the playground.

"Sometimes," Mitzi said, on the way home, "you have to tell a little white lie or two. That kid is never going to bother Theodore again."

This time I knew she was telling the truth.

sixteen

The Telegram

We stopped at Mitzi's house on the way home from the schoolyard to see if there was a letter from Buddy in the afternoon mail. As we approached the entrance, we could see little clusters of neighbors standing in the lobby. Some of the women were still wearing their aprons, as if they had rushed away from their kitchens without thinking. There was a loud hum of conversation that faded as we came closer, and I could see that a few of the people were crying.

"What happened?" Mitzi asked. "What happened, Mrs. Applebaum?"

The woman she questioned wiped her eyes with the corner of her apron, but she didn't answer.

"Ah, poor little girl," another woman said, shaking her head.

"But what is it?" Mitzi asked. "Oh, please tell me . . . what's happened?"

The man who was the Blooms' next-door neighbor came over and took Mitzi's hand. "Try to have courage, dear," he said. "Maybe everything will be all right."

"Is it my brother?" she said, in a voice so thin I could hardly hear her.

Mrs. Applebaum crossed her arms. "War!" she said, in an angry voice. "If women ran the world, if *mothers* were in charge, there wouldn't be any wars!"

Mitzi had turned white, and she was trembling as if she were standing in a cold wind. "Is . . . he . . . is . . . he . . . ?" She couldn't bring herself to ask that terrible question. I opened *my* mouth but no sound came out at all.

"There was a telegram from the War Department," one of the men said at last. "Missing in action."

Mitzi fell to the floor before anyone could reach out to catch her. There was a lot of noise and everyone rushed around her. I knelt down and rubbed her hand. "Oh,

Mitzi!" I begged. "Please get up!"

Finally one of the men lifted her in his arms and carried her upstairs. I followed right behind him. When we got to her apartment, I felt almost afraid to go inside. Mr. Bloom came to the door and helped the other man put Mitzi on the living-room sofa. His face was gray and his hands trembled. I could see the telegram lying on the floor next to the coffee table. On the table was a photograph of Buddy in his Army uniform, his eyes smiling, the rest of his face trying to look serious.

Mitzi opened her eyes and looked around, surprised to find herself in her own apartment. Then I guess she remembered the terrible news about Buddy and she burst into tears. "Oh, Daddy!" she cried, and she and her father put their arms around each other. Two other neighbors looked out at us from the bedroom, where Mrs. Bloom must have been lying down.

I couldn't think of anything to say to Mitzi or her father. I felt so awful, very shaky, and my teeth were chattering. I leaned over and put my cheek against Mitzi's and then I went out of the apartment and downstairs. Buddy, I thought as I walked home. Oh, don't let it be true. I thought of Buddy's face, the way his cheeks dimpled when he smiled. I thought of the letter he sent me. Dear Peewee. I remembered how he always whistled coming up the stairs, how his mother could tell it was him even before the door opened. I began to run on my rubbery legs, wanting more than anything else to be home again.

Mother took one look at me and walked me right into my bedroom. She pulled off my shoes and tucked the blankets around me without saying anything. I looked at her, feeling like a baby again, little and wordless. She held my hand. "I know, darling," she said. "I know. Mrs. Greene just told me. Oh, what an awful war!"

Velma and Theodore stood in the doorway, staring as if I had some terrible and contagious disease.

Then Daddy came home from work, and he and Mother went into the kitchen together and whispered for a while. I kept thinking of Buddy, remembering the newsreels at the Loew's. All that gunfire, all those explosions of light. I remembered the soldiers digging foxholes and jumping into them, the tanks rolling across the hills, the airplanes roaring over and the bombs dropping.

I must have slept because I opened my eyes and saw Theodore in his pajamas, sitting up in bed. He looked frightened and he was staring at me as if he thought I might be dead. I tried to smile at him, but I think it was a lopsided smile.

Daddy came in then and sat on the edge of my bed. He took his eyeglasses off and he rubbed his eyes. "We have to be hopeful, Shirley-girl. Buddy may be all right. Sometimes men who are missing in action turn up later, just separated from their battalions, or he might even be a prisoner of the enemy. We can only wait and see."

"B-but it's such an awful war!" I said, remembering that my mother had said the same thing a few hours before.

Theodore came over and sat on Daddy's lap. "All wars are awful," Daddy said, stroking Theodore's head. "Always remember that, sport."

Then I had a terrible thought. What if Theodore was finally cured of being a sissy? What if he became courageous and gallant, only to grow up and fight in another war someday? It was the worst thought I had ever had.

Daddy put Theodore back into his own bed and covered him. "Sleep tight, sport," he said, leaning over to kiss him. Then he came back to my bed and kissed me too.

Mother came into the room with a glass of warm milk for me. "You missed your supper tonight," she said. "Drink this, Shirley. You'll feel better and it will help you to sleep."

I wasn't really hungry, not in a good way at least, but my empty stomach rumbled and roared. My mother and father stood together in the doorway, watching me drink the milk, and it was warm and sweet going down.

seventeen

Embarrassment

The spelling bee to determine the best speller in Brooklyn was to be held in Borough Hall. The winner would compete in the final contest to find the best speller in all of New York City. When I woke up that Saturday morning I felt tired and sad, not nervous and excited the way I'd felt before the other bees.

"What's the matter?" my mother asked as she pulled the window shades up.

The sun rushed in and I hid my head under the covers.

"I don't feel so good," I said, from that dark place under my quilt.

"What? I can't hear you under there."

"I don't think I feel so good," I said, peeking out.

"Open your mouth," my mother said. "Stick out your tongue."

"My throat doesn't hurt."

"Then what is it? Is it your stomach?"

I shook my head. "It's just a *feeling*." I couldn't think of any other way to explain it.

Mother sat down on Theodore's empty bed. I could hear him talking to Velma and Daddy in the kitchen. "I'm sorry that Daddy and I can't go with you today," Mother said. "You know we have to go to see Grandpa. He's so sick. But we'll be with you in spirit anyway. And Velma and Theodore will be there to represent the family."

"I know," I said, sitting up and hugging my knees. But nothing was the same any more. The spelling bee wasn't as important to me. There had been no news about Buddy since that telegram two weeks before. Mitzi wasn't going to be at the spelling bee either. I hardly saw her after school any more, because she rushed home every afternoon to be with her mother.

As if she could read my thoughts, Mother said, "Even if Mitzi isn't there, I'm sure she'd want you to do your best. Buddy would too, you know. And Miss Cohen will be counting on you. You represent P.S. 247 today, Shirley, not just yourself."

I got up then and ate my breakfast, even though I wasn't very hungry. Theodore and Velma and I went to the bus stop together.

"Don't be nervous," Velma said, acting nervous herself. She kept hopping from one foot to the other and looking down the street every few seconds to see if the bus was coming. "Do you want me to test you?" she asked, when we were on the bus heading downtown.

"No, thank you," I said, and for the rest of the ride I just looked out the window as we rode through Brooklyn.

The borough president kept smiling and smiling. Photographers took pictures of him sitting alone at his big desk and more pictures of all the kids in the spelling bee standing around him while he pretended to write something on a blank piece of paper. Then we all went to a small auditorium. Miss Cohen was there and she was wearing a corsage of yellow roses on her shoulder. Dr. Vanderbilt sat with the other principals. He winked at me when I took my place on the stage.

The borough president cleared his throat as one last flashbulb popped. "Ladies and gentlemen," he said. "This is an auspicious occasion. 'Auspicious'—I'm sure you all know how to spell *that!*"

Everyone laughed politely.

"Seriously," he said. "We have every reason to be proud of these boys and girls who stand before us today. They have come through with flying colors against very strong competition. They represent their schools, their districts, and their fine and dedicated teachers. Good luck to all of you!"

I looked into the audience. I could see Velma and Theodore sitting in the second row with the families of the other contestants. Velma waved at me and smiled, and I nodded.

There were seven boys and five girls in the bee this time. They came from all the different school districts of Brooklyn and I had never seen any of them before.

The words were easy in the beginning, just as they had been in the other bees. No one was eliminated during the first five rounds. The borough president wiped his forehead with a handkerchief. "I'm afraid *I* would have been out of the running a long time ago," he said, and then he continued. The audience was very, very quiet.

Finally one of the boys was eliminated on the word "souvenir." Then two kids in a row had trouble with "pachyderm." One by one, contestants were eliminated until there were only three of us left, one boy and two girls. I was in the middle.

"Try to relax," the borough president said. "We all

recognize the tremendous pressure on you boys and girls. You're doing a fine job." Then he turned to the last boy. " 'Syllable,' " he said. "The accent is on the second *syllable*. 'Syllable.' "

The boy shifted from one foot to the other and looked out at the audience for a moment. " 'Syllable,' " he said, in a squeaky voice. Then he spelled it very slowly and carefully, but he still left out one of the *l*'s.

It was up to me. " 'Syllable,' " I said, and then I spelled it correctly. The boy took a seat with the other students who had been eliminated. The remaining girl and I looked at each other shyly and we smiled.

"Well," said the borough president. "One of you young ladies is the best speller in all of Brooklyn. In a few moments we will know who she is. May I take this opportunity to say that all of you are fine spellers and splendid citizens of our wonderful Borough of Brooklyn!" There was a little applause from the audience and then it was quiet again.

The other girl and I spelled "chivalrous," "hibernation," "deferment," "illuminate," and "luncheon."

Then it was my turn again and the word was "embarrassment."

I tried to picture the word inside my head, to think of the way it would look on paper. I couldn't remember if there were two *r*'s or only one. It didn't seem right no matter how I spelled it. Everyone was waiting for me to say something. The other girl had her hands clasped tightly at her waist.

I took a deep breath. "E," I said, "m-b-a-r"—everyone was looking at me, waiting for me to continue— "a-s-s-m-e-n-t."

"I'm sorry, Miss Braverman," the borough president said. "That is not correct. Please wait and we will see if Miss Halloran can spell it correctly."

Miss Halloran could. A great cheer went up from the audience after she put in both *r*'s and *s*'s. The photographers were there again taking pictures. I shook hands with the girl who'd won and I forced myself to smile when people rushed up to congratulate her.

Then Miss Cohen and Dr. Vanderbilt were there too. "You did extremely well for P.S. 247," he said, and he didn't seem disappointed at all. Neither did Miss Cohen. "You were wonderful, Shirley." She hugged me and the corsage of roses was crushed between us.

"Well, I lost," I said.

"Not at all. You came in second," Miss Cohen said, as if there was a difference. "You're the runner-up. It's a great honor."

I didn't think it was such a great honor. Somebody else was going to be the best speller in New York City. Somebody else was going to wear the mayor's medal. I wished I could just lie down on the floor and cry.

Miss Cohen opened her pocketbook and took out a small package, beautifully wrapped in silver paper and blue ribbon. "This is a little present from me," she said. "For trying so hard and for caring so much about words. Go ahead, Shirley, open it."

I sighed and then I pulled the bow on the blue ribbon and carefully opened the silver paper. There was a small red leather book inside. All the pages were blank, but on the cover MY THOUGHTS was printed in gold. My eyes filled with tears, making the words run together.

"Please listen to me, Shirley," Miss Cohen said. "I bought this for you, not knowing whether you would win today or not. I bought it because I want you to know that there's something more important about words than just spelling them correctly. We use words to tell other people how we feel, the way that authors do in the books we love. I hope you'll write *your* thoughts and feelings down. Who knows—maybe someday you'll write a real book too, one that everyone will want to read."

"Thank you, Miss Cohen," I managed to say, but I didn't feel better at all. It was true that I loved to read, but I had never thought about being a writer myself. All I could think of was that I had lost the spelling bee, no matter what Miss Cohen said, no matter what anyone said. Embarrassment. It was the worst word in the English language.

Theodore and Velma and I went home on the bus together and I could tell that they hardly knew what to say to me. Velma kept talking about her shoes and how they pinched her toes and about the fact that it looked like rain. Theodore didn't say anything at all.

When we got home, I put the little red leather book in the hall closet with all the other things I hardly ever used.

Embarrassment, I thought. I knew I would always blush when I heard that word.

eighteen
Another Telegram

Mitzi wasn't home when the *second* telegram from the War Department came, either. She and I had gone to the park for the morning because her mother had insisted. "All the roses are gone from your cheeks," Mrs. Bloom said sadly. "You hardly look like my Mitzi any more. I want you to get out in the fresh air and sunshine."

"But what if . . ." Mitzi began.

"No more whats and no more ifs," her mother said firmly. "Go to the park with Shirley and don't come home again a minute before twelve o'clock. Then you can both have lunch here together. Go ahead now. I'll be all right for a few hours without you."

The two of us left for the park then, but Mitzi kept looking back over her shoulder at her mother waving from the window.

The war in Europe was almost over. Everyone said so, and it was on the radio and in the newspapers. The Allies were winning, but there was still no word from Buddy. Missing in action. Lost. I remembered when Theodore was lost at the beach once and how we all walked up and down the shore calling his name. My mother wrung her hands and looked out at the ocean with one hand shading her eyes. Theodore was only a baby then and the waves were big. Then we heard the lifeguard's whistle and we looked up to see him holding Theodore high in the air.

I tried again to cheer Mitzi up. Her mother was right, she *was* pale and her hair and eyes seemed to have lost their shine. "Come on!" I said. "I'll race you." Mitzi, with her long, thin legs, who always beat me in every kind of race, was lagging far behind when I arrived, panting, at the entrance to the playground.

It was a place where we'd played since we were little kids, a place where we had been pushed on the baby swings by our fathers and been caught in our mothers' arms at the end of the long slide.

That day we went on the seesaw together, up and down in the sunlight. I bumped down hard every time my end of it touched the ground, making Mitzi bounce in the air a little, her hair flying up. It was something she had always liked, but this time she just sat there, as if riding on a seesaw weren't any different from sitting in an armchair at home.

On the swings I pumped myself high, until I felt as if my feet would touch the rooftops outside the park and even the clouds above them. It was such a beautiful spring day that it was hard to believe it wasn't as sweet and peaceful everywhere in the world. Mitzi just let her swing dangle while the toes of her shoes scraped against the ground.

"Do you want a push?" I asked. She shook her head sadly.

I knew she really wanted to go home, that there wasn't anything in the park that could interest her when she was feeling so bad. But we had promised her mother we would stay until lunchtime.

We left the playground area and walked to the grassy section of the park, where there was a grove of trees blooming with new leaves. Mitzi and I lay down in their shadow. There was a patch of clover near me and I searched carefully, hoping I'd find one with four leaves. Mitzi was pretty superstitious and she thought that four-leaf clovers could bring you good luck. If I found one I was going to give it to her. But there seemed to be a million of them with three leaves or five and not one with just four. I thought of tearing one leaf off a five-leaf clover and pretending I had really found a four-leaf clover, but somehow I couldn't do it.

Neither of us had a watch but we knew that when the sun was directly overhead it would be noon and we could start back again.

"Do you want to play Ghost?" I asked.

Mitzi shook her head.

"Geography?"

Another head shake.

"Actors and Actresses?"

I didn't want to play any of those games myself but I felt we had to keep busy until it was time to go back to Mitzi's house. I didn't know any new Knock Knocks or riddles or jokes. Mitzi was the one who always told them to me and she hadn't told me any for weeks.

"Shut your eyes," I said, "and try to count to a million. Maybe then it will be time to go home."

We were both quiet for a long time.

"What are you up to?" I asked.

"Four hundred and sixty-two," Mitzi said, and she sighed. "Let's go ask that man what time it is."

There was an old man sitting on a bench reading a

newspaper. He looked at his watch and he told Mitzi that it was eleven o'clock.

"See?" I told Mitzi. "Only one more hour."

"A whole hour," Mitzi said, sighing again. We sat there for a while, not saying anything, just poking at the clover.

Then Mitzi got up again and asked the old man to tell her the time. He stared at her and rattled his newspaper. "*Five* after eleven," he said.

Mitzi came back and sat down. "I think his watch stopped," she whispered. "Let's walk up to the jewelry store on the parkway and see what time it really is."

We tried to take our time, but when we got to the jewelry store and looked at the big clock in the window, it was only ten after eleven. "I don't believe it," Mitzi said. "What are we going to do?"

We finally decided to walk up and down the parkway looking in the store windows until it was twelve o'clock. We would keep going back to the jewelry store to check the time.

Window-shopping was something that Mitzi and I always liked. Sometimes we would pretend to be grown-ups thinking of buying new furniture for our homes, or a Frigidaire. We would look in the beauty parlor and pretend that we were going to get our hair dyed red or our nails manicured. And of course we didn't have to pretend at all when we looked in the window of the Marlboro Toy and Game Shop.

But this time it was different. Nothing really interested us, not even the beautiful smells of fresh bread and cake from the open bakery door. And it was not even eleven-thirty when we got back to the jewelry store again.

"Let's go home right now, Shirley," Mitzi said.

I hesitated. "It's not time yet."

"We'll walk very slow-ly," Mitzi said, lifting one foot carefully in the air and setting it down again in slow motion.

"But your mother . . . and the fresh air . . ."

"I've had *enough* fresh air!" Mitzi shouted. "I'm choking on all this fresh air!"

So we went home, and not so slowly after all. When we got to Mitzi's house, we found Mrs. Bloom waiting at the door to their apartment. "Where *were* you?" she said. "I thought you were going to the park! Your father looked *everywhere* for you!"

Mitzi opened her mouth, but before she could speak, her father appeared in the doorway. "You're home! Well, what do you think of the news, eh? Isn't it wonderful?" He picked Mitzi up in his arms as if she were a baby and he swung her around and around.

"*What* news?" she shouted to him from somewhere near the ceiling.

Her father put her down again slowly. "Your brother," he said.

Mitzi looked at her mother, who just smiled and nodded her head, her eyes shining with tears.

"Your brother," her father said again. "He's safe!"

Mitzi and I looked at each other without speaking. I felt weak with happiness and surprise.

Then the Blooms showed us the second telegram from the War Department. Buddy had been taken prisoner by the enemy and the Allies had just liberated the camp where he had been held. He would probably be home in a few weeks!

The Blooms wanted me to stay and have lunch with Mitzi but both of us were too excited to eat, and I wanted to rush home and tell my family the wonderful news.

At the door Mitzi rapped lightly on my forehead with her fist. "Knock knock," she said.

"Who's there," I asked.

"Mitzi."

"Mitzi who?"

"Mitzi Bloom," she said. "That's me, the happiest girl in America!"

nineteen
Cure No. 3: Theodore in the Basement

Grandpa Small died in his sleep one night and the funeral was going to be held the next day. Mother and Daddy decided that Theodore was too young to attend and that I would have to stay home with him. Velma was going to go to the services with them.

On the morning of the funeral everyone dressed quietly. Velma looked very strange wearing an ugly green hat she had borrowed from Aunt Lena. Mother wore a black dress and Daddy put on his darkest suit.

There were tears in Mother's eyes and every once in a while she sat down in a chair and just stared ahead of her as if she was trying to remember something. Daddy spoke to her in a soft voice and she began to cry. Theodore looked worried and he sucked on his finger while he watched Mother.

At last it was time for them to leave. Mother wore a hat too and she was very pale. Daddy and Velma each held one of her arms as they went down the hall.

Theodore and I ran to the window and saw them drive away in a long black limousine.

Then we were all alone in the apartment and it had never seemed so quiet. Theodore kept following me around from room to room. Finally he said, "Why is Mommy doing that?"

"She's very sad," I told him. "She'll never see her father again."

"Then where are they g-going?"

"To the funeral," I said, trying to imagine what a funeral was actually like. "That's where they say prayers, like he should rest in peace and he should go to heaven."

Theodore was thoughtful for a moment, probably thinking about heaven. He even went back to the window and looked up at the sky. Then he came back and sat down next to me. "H-how does it feel to be d-dead?" he wanted to know.

"Oh, it's nothing," I told him. "They just can't move any more. You know, they can't eat or talk or anything. So they dig a big hole and put them in a box. Then they put the box in the hole."

"Why c-can't they k-keep him?"

I thought about that for a moment. "Because he would smell bad," I said.

"Oh."

We were both quiet for a few minutes. In a way I wished they had allowed Theodore to go to the funeral. For one wild moment I had even imagined they would let us see our dead grandfather, and although the idea really scared me, I thought *this* might be Theodore's cure. To look in the face of a dead man. Maybe even to *touch* him. But here we were, alone in the apartment, while everyone else was at the funeral.

I thought of Mother again and the way she always spoke about Grandpa Small, about how handsome he was, and lively. I tried hard to imagine Mother as a little girl skating in the park with Grandpa Small, who had been her father. For a moment I felt that I could almost see them, their red scarves flying out behind them as they skated by. For the first time I really believed her! I knew it was possible that Grandpa Small *had* been young and handsome once, and now he was dead. My mother would never see her father again. A sad feeling spread in my throat and my chest.

"A-and he'll never come b-back?" Theodore asked.

"Never."

"Really n-never?"

"Never ever never ever."

"Not even as a g-ghost?" he persisted.

"Oh, Theodore!" I was exasperated. How, *how* would I ever see him through this cowardice? I stared at him. An idea was growing inside my head. "Listen," I said. "Let's go outside. It's too warm in here." It was true. The weather was getting warmer with the change of seasons and the apartment seemed hot and airless.

But when we went downstairs the sun was bright and blinding. "What do you want to do?" Theodore asked, squinting in the brightness. A rash of prickly heat sprinkled his neck and his forehead.

"I don't know. What do *you* want to do?"

"Let's go back upstairs," Theodore said.

"I've got an idea," I said. "Let's go where it's nice and cool."

"W-where?"

"Oh," I said casually, "let's go downstairs."

"In the b-basement?" He looked at me as if I were crazy.

"Sure," I said. "Listen, it's always cooler in a basement, isn't it? We'll just go downstairs to get ourselves good and cool and then we'll come right back up again. I'll teach you a good card game later, when we come back up." I crossed my arms and tucked my hands under my armpits. My fingers were icy.

Theodore was rubbing his eyes. "I don't w-wanna go," he said.

"Oh, why do you want to be such a baby!" I said. "C'mon, Theodore," I added in a sweeter voice. "I'll make you a nice soda later."

"N-no!" He started to cry.

"Okay," I said. "Don't go. See if I care. But when they come home, I'll tell Daddy that you were lighting matches."

"B-but I didn't!"

He looked so awful, so surprised and disappointed, that I almost changed my mind. But I remembered that it was all for his own good. "I'll tell them anyway," I said in a mean voice.

I watched Theodore as he thought it over. He started to suck on his finger again. He kicked at the curb with the toe of his shoe. "All right," he said sadly.

"See! See!" I shouted. "You're not such a baby!"

I took his hand and we walked to the side of the building, where a black iron railing ran alongside the basement ramp. In a moment we were at the heavy door that led to the basement. A yellow sign with an arrow on it said Air Raid Shelter. I pulled the door open and we stepped inside. It snapped closed behind us and there was an awful echo. The walls of the basement were rough and they were painted gray. Very small light bulbs hung close to the low ceiling. We could stare right at them without blinking or seeing floating colors. It was pretty damp in the basement but it really was much cooler. The passageway was narrow and curving and at the first turn we came to the room that we always used during air-raid drills. It was dark in there now, and without anyone in it, the room seemed gloomy and strange. We kept walking until we came to two long rows of stalls, narrow cages with wooden bars across them. Each one was fastened with a lock, and was marked with a letter and a number. These were the bins where the tenants of every apartment were allowed to store their things. In the dim light I could read 1B, 3F, 5C. We saw bicycles with rusty chains and peeling paint. There were the shapes of baby carriages covered with rubber sheets or smelly oilcloth. There were labeled cartons and old steamer trunks. Then we came to a bin marked 2G and I nudged Theodore. "This is ours," I said proudly, as if I had discovered some wonderful family secret. I reached in between the wooden slats and lifted one corner of a gray rubber sheet and there was Theodore's old carriage. I rocked it and the springs creaked and whined. "Look, look," I told him. "It was *yours!* Do you remember? I used to wheel you in it." Something rattled inside the carriage and I searched with one hand along the cold leather lining and pulled out a string of faded wooden beads. I placed them over his head and laughed, but Theodore pulled them off and threw them into a dark corner of the basement.

"I w-want to go back up!" he said.

"But we didn't even see anything yet! We hardly even went inside. Come on. Let's go find the place where the coal comes in down the chute."

I took his hand. It was wet and I wiped it against the front of his polo shirt. I began to lead him down the passageway again. There were words written on the walls, proof of other real and harmless people who had been there before us. They had written "H.L. & M.W." inside a heart, "Jerry was here," and "Max & Faye forever!" We came to a door that was painted bright red and marked DANGER, and we ran quickly past it. Suddenly a humming noise began and we both stood very still and listened.

"W-what's *that*?" Theodore whispered.

"I don't know," I admitted. "But it must be something that makes things go inside the house. Like the water or the lights or something." We had passed large mysterious wall switches and fat dusty pipes, so my explanation seemed to make sense, even to me. Now we moved past more doors that were bolted with heavy locks and for one terrible moment all the lights flickered. Theodore made a small moaning sound in his throat.

"A little more," I coaxed. "A little more and then we'll go upstairs." I was feeling pretty worried and nervous myself, and I started thinking about scary things like zombies and werewolves. But somehow I felt this cure wouldn't work unless we completed a tour of the whole basement. We made a sharp turn then and the humming noise stopped suddenly. This was more frightening than when it had started. It was so quiet. We couldn't hear anything at all. I wondered if we had come too far, if the flickering lights had been a warning to leave.

"All right," I said. "All right, we'll go back now if you want to."

"If *you* want to," Theodore said.

We turned around and followed the curve of the walls. When we reached the storage bins again, we hesitated. We peered into the one marked 3H. That was Mrs. Golub's apartment number. Carton upon carton upon carton in a tall shaky tower. We poked at them through the bars, and curls of dust floated down.

"It's probably junk," I said. "Nothing but stupid junk."

We walked to the next bin and behind us there was a slight shifting noise and some rattling, as if someone was following us. Theodore screamed and banged his head against my stomach. Then, with a thunderous explosion, the cartons in Mrs. Golub's bin came down.

Tumbling, crashing, sliding, they emptied their contents as they fell. China cups and saucers, dolls, movie magazines and photos, shoes and umbrellas fell in a crazy pile all over the bin.

We ran. I passed Theodore and then he passed me. We ran and we ran and we didn't turn around once. I came to the heavy door first and I used both hands to push it open, but Theodore raced past me and he was out first. We took giant steps up the steep ramp and stood outside again in the sunshine, panting and trembling.

"I-it's all your f-fault," he said. "Y-you made me go!"

I had to fight back the tears. "Nothing happened to *you*. Nothing happened to you, anyway. Nobody even saw us."

Theodore looked at me. "I'm going to tell," he said.

"You wouldn't."

He looked back at me without blinking. "I'm going to tell," he said again.

"Don't!" I shouted. "Don't you *dare!* Don't you dare tell!"

Theodore walked to the curb and sat down. He began to tie the lace of one of his shoes, using two loops just the way I had taught him. He didn't look up again until he was finished. "What will you give me?" he asked, without a trace of his old stutter.

That was the beginning, I guess. I knew that if he

didn't tell Mother and Daddy about what we had done, I probably would myself. Something like that could give you an awfully guilty conscience. But I didn't like him as much any more. That was the beginning. At last, Theodore was on his own.

twenty

Welcome Home!

The war in Europe was over now and we were waiting for the same news from the Pacific, where many of our men were still fighting. Buddy Bloom was coming home finally, and Mitzi and Theodore and I made big signs for all of the windows.

WELCOME HOME, BUDDY

OUR HERO

BENSONHURST WELCOMES BUDDY BLOOM

Mrs. Bloom was so nervous the day Buddy was to arrive that she kept laughing and crying and dropping everything she picked up. Mr. Bloom whistled one song after another and cut himself in four places when he shaved. At eleven o'clock Mitzi left with her parents for the pier in Manhattan where the troop transport was going to dock, bringing home thousands of men who had been prisoners of war.

Theodore and I waited on Mitzi's street with a crowd of neighbors. We all had small American flags and bags of confetti. We were planning to wave the flags and throw the confetti as soon as we saw Buddy. The Blooms were going to bring him home from the city in a taxi. Other neighbors leaned out their windows and looked up and down the street, waiting for the big moment.

When the soldiers in Buddy's prison camp were liberated, they were sent to Paris, France, to a hospital, where they were all examined. Wounded men and soldiers who were ill were going to be kept there until they were well. Buddy wrote from the hospital that he was all right and that the doctors were going to let him come home. He was just a little thinner, he wrote, but he was sure his mother could take care of that. Mrs. Bloom began cooking as soon as they received that letter. Great steaming pots of soup bubbled on her stove. Cakes and breads rose in her oven and the whole apartment was filled with the good smells of her cooking.

Now, every time Theodore saw something turn the corner, he shouted, "It's them! It's them!" and some of the neighbors began to wave their little flags and reach into their bags of confetti. But it would only be a car or a delivery truck and not the taxi at all. Then, when I turned my head the other way for a moment, Theodore shouted again, "It's them! It's them!" I was going to say something to him about the boy who cried wolf, when I looked up and saw that it *was* a taxi, a big yellow taxi coming down the street toward us. Suddenly I remembered the red rose Buddy had mentioned in his letter. I wasn't wearing one in my hair. Would he be able to recognize me after all this time?

Other people had taken up Theodore's cry. "It's them! It's them!" At the last minute, one of the men lifted Theodore up onto his shoulders, so his flag was higher than anyone else's.

When the taxi door opened and Buddy Bloom stepped out, Theodore's confetti seemed to fall from the skies like beautiful colored snow. As for me, I forgot all about the flag and the confetti, all about the wonderful speech I planned to make. I saw that tall, thin soldier look around him and that familiar smile grow on his face when he knew that he was really there, home again in Brooklyn.

I saw him open his arms wide and I heard him yell,

"Peewee, I'm home!" I rushed at him, the tears in my eyes blurring everything, and I threw my arms around him. The confetti fell on my head too, and all around us neighbors called, from windows and fire escapes, "Buddy! Welcome home, boy! Hello, Buddy! Welcome home!"

twenty-one
Moving Day

"You girls vote on a color and Daddy will buy the paint," Mother said. She dumped a carton of Velma's books on my bed.

It was moving day at our apartment, but only Velma and Theodore were moving. He was going to have Velma's little bedroom for himself and Velma and I were going to share the bigger room.

It seemed strange already without Theodore's toys all over the floor, without his trucks and cars and the little ship inside the bottle. Velma carried in some more of her things and I looked at them as if I had never seen them before. Everything did look different when you put it in a new place. We had pushed the beds and night tables around all morning until we decided where to put them.

"Blue!" Velma and I said together, when Mother asked us to vote on a color for the walls. At least we both had the same favorite color. Daddy pushed Velma's dressing table against the wall and Velma carried in the stool that went with it. I sat down on the stool and looked into the heart-shaped mirror while Velma arranged bottles of cologne and dusting powder on a flowered china tray. When she left the room again, I picked up one bottle after another, reading the names of the scents. White Shoulders, Evening in Paris, Tabu. The names were pretty stupid, but I picked up an atomizer and squeezed it and then my left arm smelled wonderful.

Everything was going to be different, I thought. For one thing, I was going to have to try to be neater or Velma and I would have some terrible fights. She had warned me that morning that she couldn't possibly sleep in a pigsty. She always liked her room to look like a picture in a magazine. Theodore never cared about things like that. When Mother made him clean things up, he would always push everything under his bed: socks, toys, empty cookie boxes. I have to admit that I never cared much either, but now with new paint and new curtains . . .

Then I wondered what would happen at night if I wanted to read and Velma wanted the lights out so she could sleep, or if she wanted to listen to her radio when *I* wanted to sleep. Theodore had always been able to sleep with the lights on *and* the radio playing, and he never said anything to me about touching his belongings or cleaning up the room.

I went down the hallway to the little bedroom that was going to be his now. Theodore was throwing a pair of his pajamas into a drawer. They were all rolled up in a ball.

"Wait a minute," I said. I folded them neatly for him, the way Velma folded hers. Then I helped him tack his picture of Lucky the dog actor over his bed. "You're really going to like this room," I told him. "It will be nice and private and special. You can decorate it any way you want to. It may be a small room, but it's nice and cozy." Secretly I believed he was going to miss me and be very lonely.

I opened another drawer and began to fold his underwear and his socks too. Then I went to the closet and opened it. Junk started falling out all over the place. "For heaven's sake, Theodore," I said. "You're a big boy now. You don't want to live in a pigsty, do you? Look at all this junk. Why don't you just throw some of this stuff out if you don't need it?" I hung his shirts on hangers and lined his shoes and sneakers up in a neat row under them. Then I looked around the room again, with my hands on my hips. "Don't you want to move your bed next to the window? Don't you want to be able to look outside in the morning without getting up?"

"No," Theodore said. "I like it over here."

"That's silly," I said. "That's the worst place. Look, your closet door is going to hit the back of the bed every time you open it. And look at those books! Theodore, you can't have books lying all over the place. Wait a minute. I'm going to let you have my nice collie-dog book ends, because I can share Velma's now. I'll be right back."

I went back to my room and began to look for the book ends. Velma was standing on her bed knocking a nail into the wall for her picture of two white kittens in a basket of wool. Mother and Daddy were measuring the windows for the new curtains. It was really going to look lovely, I thought. Mother had said we could get new bedspreads to match the curtains. We were going to the store that week to pick them out.

I looked among the cartons and books and games on the beds until I found the collie-dog book ends. I marched down the hallway again to Theodore's new room. His door was shut. I was going to knock when I saw there was a crayoned sign tacked up.

PRIVIT PROPPITY

T. BRAVERMAN

KEEP OUT

THIS MEENS YOU!

Well! I said to myself. If *that's* the way he wants it. What do I care? I would have helped him fix up a perfectly nice room, something he could have been proud of. But if he wanted to live in a pigsty, I decided, that was *his* problem. I turned around and brought the book ends back to my room.

That night, after Velma and I climbed into our beds, I thought how quiet it was and how strange it seemed to look across the room and not see Theodore, a little round lump huddled under the covers.

Velma said, "Do you want to read?"

I shook my head. "I'm too tired. Do you?"

"No. Let's talk instead."

Talk? Velma and I hardly ever talked to each other. What in the world would we talk about? "Okay," I said, a little worried that she would want to make a list of rules and regulations for keeping our room neat.

"If you want to, Shirley," Velma said, "you can use

my cologne sometimes. Evening in Paris is my favorite."

"Thank you," I said.

"And you can borrow some of my other things too," she said. "If you *ask* me first."

"All right." I remembered the mystery of Velma's dresser drawer, where the lipstick and nail polish had appeared from under a pile of underwear.

"And," Velma continued, "you can ask me things, if you want to."

"What things?"

"Oh, you know, like about problems you have. And about the birds and the bees and stuff like that."

I lay there for a while, thinking about that. There wasn't anything I wanted to ask Velma. Not yet, anyway. But I felt strangely happy. Velma was offering to be my friend. "Okay," I said, "and you can borrow some of my things too. *If* you ask me first," I added.

Later, when the lights were out all over the apartment, I turned around in my bed and looked across the room. In the moonlight I could see Velma, looking a little like a ghost because of some white lotion she put on her face every night to fight pimples. Her head was covered with shiny pink curlers and she hugged her pillow with both arms. My sister.

On the morning of August 15, we woke up and found that the war had ended. Through the open windows we could hear people calling to one another all over the neighborhood. "The war is over! Peace!"

I looked out and saw that men and women were standing in the street in their pajamas and bathrobes. Children blew on toy horns and music blasted from someone's phonograph.

Daddy came to the table for breakfast wearing his

striped pajamas and his air-raid warden's hat. "Oh, *Morris,*" my mother said, bursting into laughter. Then my father took the helmet off. He went to the sink, where Mother had a jelly glass filled with yellow roses from a neighbor's garden. He took the flowers, water and all, and put them into his upside-down helmet. He walked over to Mother, who was frying eggs in a pan, and bowed deeply. "In honor of world peace," he said to her. "Oh, Morris," Mother said again, but she smiled and took the helmet and put it on the windowsill in the sunlight.

Later in the day a committee of neighbors came over and asked my parents to help prepare for a block party to celebrate the wonderful news. Some of them made banners and strung them from the fire escapes. Others made sandwiches and punch and cake. Later that afternoon a police car arrived and two policemen put up wooden saw-horses to keep cars off our block. Then all the families brought out chairs and tables and put them right in the middle of the street! Three men with musical instruments began to tune up under our windows. Flags appeared on poles and homemade signs were hung, welcoming peace and the soldiers and sailors who were coming home.

Mitzi came over in the afternoon to help. "Knock knock," she said at the door.

"Who's there?" I asked.

"Lemmy."

"Lemmy who?"

"Lemmy in!" she said, and I opened the door. She was the same old Mitzi again.

Theodore and Velma and Mitzi and I went up and down the stairs a hundred times that day carrying folding chairs and paper tablecloths and noisemakers and platters of cake.

The band began to play and people started dancing in the street as if it were a dance floor in a nightclub. Stray dogs ran in and out between our feet looking for scraps of food, and up in the sky an airplane was spelling out V FOR VICTORY in little clouds of smoke.

Some of the old women danced together with party hats tilted on their heads. I saw Mrs. Golub dancing with the superintendent of our building. Her eyes were closed and I wondered if she was pretending that he was Clark Gable. Old Mr. Katz whirled Mrs. Katz around and around, until, laughing, she said she was dizzy and made him stop.

The party went on and on until the whole street was littered with junk, and little kids fell asleep in their mothers' arms. The musicians took a break and then they began to play again. Fathers and mothers danced their sleeping children right into the lobby of the building and upstairs, where they put them to bed. My mother and father danced, holding each other very close, and my mother had her head on my father's shoulder. The sun went down and all at once the street lights went on. The band played a song called "When the Lights Go on Again All over the World" and everyone applauded and whistled. I was so sleepy. It had been the happiest day of my life and I wished that I could stay up forever.

But finally I climbed the stairs to our apartment. Theodore was fast asleep in his room with all his clothes on. I went to the window and looked out. In the distance I could hear firecrackers going off and music from other streets mixing with the music from ours. There was only one couple still dancing. Some of the other people were starting to fold tables and chairs and a man was sweeping the street with a big push broom.

I went to the hall closet and looked and looked until I found the red notebook that Miss Cohen had given me the day I lost the spelling bee. I took a pencil from a drawer in the kitchen and I sat down near the window so I could hear all the last wonderful noises of the party. I opened the book to the first page and in my best handwriting I wrote: "I am twelve years old and I live in Brooklyn, New York. Today the war ended."